"Where are you going?"

"None of your business."

"Why? Is it a secret?" She 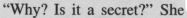 just before it spoke, a green light blinked beneath the speaker on its side.

This time the robot did not answer. Instead, its metal feet scraped for traction against the crumbling pavement and it walked forward. The robot lurched a little with every other step. After climbing a few yards it stopped again. She was going to ask if it wanted a push but hesitated; she didn't feel like hearing another lecture.

A song sparrow lit on the turret and immediately flew off again. The turret moved as the camera eyes watched the bird fly first to a blueberry bush and then to the branch of a young maple tree just coming into leaf. Then the bird paused to sing a brief sweet song before flitting off again into the pine thicket. With a distinct sigh the robot moved on.

She'd never heard a robot sigh.

Don't get left behind!

STARSCAPE
Let the journey begin . . .

From the Two Rivers
  The Eye of the World: Part One
  by Robert Jordan

To the Blight
  The Eye of the World: Part Two
  by Robert Jordan

Ender's Game
  by Orson Scott Card

The Cockatrice Boys
  by Joan Aiken

Briar Rose
  by Jane Yolen

Dogland
  by Will Shetterly

Mairelon the Magician
  by Patricia C. Wrede

The Whispering Mountain
  by Joan Aiken

Ender's Shadow
  by Orson Scott Card

The Garden Behind the Moon
  by Howard Pyle

And look for . . .

The Dark Side of Nowhere (7/02)
  by Neal Shusterman

Deep Secret (11/02)
  by Diana Wynne Jones

Prince Ombra (8/02)
  by Roderick MacLeish

Pinocchio (11/02)
  by Carlo Collodi

The Magician's Ward (9/02)
  by Patricia C. Wrede

*Another Heaven, Another
  Earth* (12/02)
  by H. M. Hoover

The College of Magics (10/02)
  by Caroline Stevermer

ORVIS

H. M. HOOVER

A TOM DOHERTY ASSOCIATES BOOK
NEW YORK

This is a work of fiction. All the characters and events portrayed in this book are either products of the author's imagination or are used fictitiously.

ORVIS

A Starscape Book
Published by Tom Doherty Associates, LLC
175 Fifth Avenue
New York, NY 10010

www.starscapebooks.com

ISBN: 0-812-55735-2

First Starscape Edition: June 2002

Printed in the Untied States of America

0 9 8 7 6 5 4 3 2 1

ORVIS

ONE

On a gray afternoon in April Toby West sat crying in a thicket. She hadn't intended to cry; the sobs just sneaked up on her as she ran. Embarrassed by this weakness, she knew that if anyone saw her and asked what was wrong, she would cry harder and humiliate herself completely. Not answering would be too dramatic. She hated dramatics and so had chosen to hide.

It was cold just sitting. The dampness of the rotting log was seeping through the seat of her pants. The backs of her legs were being poked by a stiff yellow fungus that grew in fanlike steps up the dead bark.

"This is stupid," she told herself sternly and sat erect. She hadn't cried all the other times. Crying wouldn't help now. If her grandmother Lillian said she had to change schools, she had to change schools. Lillian was The Boss and her word was law to Toby's parents. So Toby would say good-bye to everyone and move again. She was so tired of saying good-bye.

When not crying, Toby was a good-looking child. Her dark hair went nicely with her tan skin. She had an acceptable nose and a determined chin. Her ears had once stuck out too far but her grandmother had had that corrected shortly after her birth. Sometimes her expression made adults uneasy; they suspected she understood too much for her age, which was twelve. But all adults agreed that her eyes were her best feature—large, dark, and fringed by long curly black lashes. Crying made her eyes puffy.

More tears welled up and spilled over. With an already damp wad of tissues she mopped her face and blew her nose, determined to regain self-control. Just as she sniffed she heard a strange sound. She held her breath to listen and absent-mindedly pocketed the tissue wad.

CRee-ECH. CRee-ECH-clack! CRee-ECH.

The noise was metallic, rhythmic, and coming closer. Probably some of the ground crew cleaning up dead branches. They might see her and wonder what she was doing out here, alone. She got up, brushed off the seat of her pants, and looked around. No workmen were in sight.

At the top of the long slope the walls and the white buildings of the Academy were visible through the trees. There was cheering in the distance; the Saturday afternoon game was in progress. Two boys were running on the track that encircled the parklike campus. When they had rounded the bend and their backs were to her, she pushed her way out of the thicket. Down the hill, to the left, something was moving. She pulled aside a laurel branch for a better view.

A lone robot came walking down the road. It had six legs like an insect and no faceplate but only a turret like half a ball where an insect's head would be. The half ball was studded with lenses and bristled with sensor wires. With every third step a leg screeched. It was limping, Toby thought. Halfway up the hill it stopped.

She had never seen so old a robot. Even in pictures all but the most ancient had wheels or airfloats, and the biometal arms were at least sheathed. Modern rover units resembled sleek shopvacs; some of the luxury servo-models were almost human in appearance, but she could not guess what this robot had been designed to do. It looked . . . *utilitarian* was the word that came to mind.

She had never liked robots—they made her ill at ease—but this one was somehow appealing. It looked like what it was, a machine. In her experience that sort of simple honesty was rare in both things and people. She ran down the hill for a closer view, dodging bushes and briars, and settled on her haunches to study the thing.

Up close it looked even older, less buglike but still awesome. The body had been painted brown. The paint was worn and chipped. Patches of yellow, silver, and dirty orange showed through dents and scratches. Any flat space on its back was covered with ring marks as if people had set wet cans and glasses there. The body was lumpy with housings, oblongs, domes, and protruding rods. There had once been hair-thin sensor wires around each foot; only a few remained intact, the rest broken off to stubby whiskers. The left rear leg was bent, two other legs didn't match in color, and the right middle foot had lost two toes. There was no manufacturer's nameplate on the unit and no owner's license. A permit was taped to the middle but Toby couldn't read the small print.

The robot stood completely still. She couldn't hear so much as a hum. Maybe it was broken? Or dead? Did robots die? Maybe it was so old it had worn out right here? Not that traffic would be bothered. No one used the road much anymore.

Intended as a bikeway, the road meandered over what had once been scenic countryside but was now hilly woodland dotted with open spaces around the ruins of empty towns. From the air at night the lights of Hillandale Academy were the only sign of human habitation for miles.

Made bold by the robot's silence, Toby stood up and went closer. The permit on its side was for temporary travel, allowing the machine ten days to walk from one place to another. Both "To" and "From" were given as numbers. The permit had expired three days before, which meant the robot was breaking a law by being here.

"Where is it going?" she wondered aloud, slowly circling the machine. "How did it get lost?"

"I am not lost." The words were distinct, coming from a meshed speaker on its side.

"What a funny voice," she said, wondering if she should be afraid. Every robot she'd ever heard spoke in mellow human tones and was inhumanly polite. This one spoke as she thought a machine should—in a brisk monotone.

"Have I made rude personal remarks about you?" said the robot. "Have I objected to being stared at and examined like a *thing*? Have I speculated aloud on your competence to judge me? Have I asked why your eyes are red, swollen, and unattractive?"

"No, but . . ." Robots weren't supposed to notice things like that, let alone question humans about them.

"I speak as I do because I am a robot," the machine went on, "not an amusing adult toy. A robot. A highly sophisticated tool of human manufacture. Humans smile to avert threat. Robots threaten humans but robots cannot smile. To reassure humans, robots are now programmed to communicate in tones which humans associate with gentleness and caring. My design suits my function."

Toby frowned. She'd never thought one way or the other about why robots spoke as they did. What this one said made sense; people *were* afraid of robots, especially if they suspected the robot was smarter than they were. Almost all robots were stronger. People said robots could do only what they were programmed to do—but no one she knew really believed that. Everyone had heard of robots who had hurt or killed people—not always by accident. This robot was big enough to be quite dangerous.

"That's very interesting," she said politely. "I didn't mean to insult you. I thought you'd broken down. Or were lost. Not much traffic comes this way. What are you doing here?"

The robot took so long to answer that she had decided

it wasn't going to when at last it said, "Delaying the in-
evitable."

"What does that mean?"

"You are not required to understand. You are a random
chance."

Vaguely insulted but curious, she persisted. "Where are
you going?"

"None of your business."

"Why? Is it a secret?" She'd noticed that just before it
spoke, a green light blinked beneath the speaker on its side.

This time the robot did not answer. Instead, its metal feet
scraped for traction against the crumbling pavement and it
walked forward. Watching how it moved fascinated her;
three feet always touched the ground so that the body was
supported at all times by a firm tripod—or would have
been, had that middle foot been intact. As it was, the robot
lurched a little with every other step. After climbing a few
yards it stopped again. She was going to ask if it wanted a
push but hesitated; she didn't feel like hearing another lecture.

A song sparrow lit on the turret and immediately flew
off again. The turret moved as the camera eyes watched
the bird fly first to a blueberry bush and then to the branch
of a young maple tree just coming into leaf. Then the bird
paused to sing a brief sweet song before flitting off
again into the pine thicket. With a distinct sigh the robot
moved on.

She'd never heard a robot sigh. How odd, she thought,
and followed, but at a respectful distance.

At the top of the grade where the road was almost a tunnel through the encroaching trees the robot stopped again. Its turret rotated an inch to the right. "Do you intend to harm me?" it said.

"No."

"Why are you following me?"

"I'm not," she lied. "I'm going to the dump."

"The Corona Landfill?"

"Yes." That name sounded vaguely familiar. "The people here call it The Dump."

"Is your design obsolete?"

"What?"

"Is your design obsolete?"

Understanding dawned. "Is yours?"

"I was judged obsolete and of use to no one."

"Who said so?"

"The probate court."

She didn't know what a probate court was, but didn't want to appear ignorant just as she might learn something. "What were you designed to be? To do?"

"I am a multi-purpose unit. I can even do windows."

"Oh." The ancient humor escaped her. "How old are you?"

At the front of the body yellow, green, and mauve lights began to blink slowly while in the middle a row of blue dots went on and off before the green slit beneath its speaker flashed on. "I do not know. Some of my processors are antique. My subsystems were replaced completely. My relational data base has been modified repeatedly as have the sequential and logical inference bases. My time and distance meters were repeatedly reset. I have been sold five times and have out-performed three of my owners."

"Out-performed them?"

"Their units ceased to function."

"They died?"

"Yes."

"Is that what happened to your last owner?"

"Yes." The robot began to move again.

"Why didn't anybody want you?"

"The consensus of three used-robot-android dealers was that my age and appearance would make my resale in today's market improbable if not impossible. One dealer said I would scare away customers if I sat on his lot. My component parts are incompatible with any modern system; therefore, I have no salvage value. No one was interested in hauling me away for scrap."

"I'm so sorry," she said and meant it, and then felt silly at having expressed sympathy to a thing with no feelings. "So they programmed you to walk here to the dump?"

"I was ordered to walk here. Yes."

"Why this dump? Why not one close to wherever it is you came from?"

Before she could ask where that was the robot had stopped again, two of its feet off the ground. Perhaps it was her imagination, but it seemed to her that the machine was exasperated.

"Because I am potentially dangerous. If I am now obsolete and unwanted, I was once and remain a high-quality unit, built to last. The same quality that went into my construction also went into my fuel cell, which, barring damage to the housing, will function as long as I can obtain water for it and without water will retain a half-life for a further twenty-five thousand years. If my component parts were as energy-efficient as my fuel cell, I would be immortal. I was ordered to proceed to this *dump*, as you so inelegantly call it, because this area is isolated. Disuse of the area assures relative safety from ignorant human scavengers who might be harmed should they attempt to dismantle me in my soon-to-be dormant state. Does that answer all your questions?"

"No. Do you have to do what you're told?"

A red bar and then a rainbow of lights blinked on as it considered this question. "I was given no alternative. Logic suggested that unwanted machines are scrap. I am unwanted."

"But you don't want to be scrap, do you? Otherwise you wouldn't be three days late getting here."

Again she thought she heard a sigh. "Robots are machines," it said. "Robots have no wants, no feelings. I am an old and slow machine."

She thought this over. "Do you breathe?"

"No."

"Then how can you sigh?"

"I do not sigh."

"You do. I heard you. Like this." She imitated the sound.

"That resembles a noise made by a previous owner when he wished to indicate a sense of minor stress or anxiety. I may mimic his sound, due to a faulty memory."

She didn't believe that but didn't want to argue. They walked on in silence, side by side, an odd pair. She was just tall enough to see across the robot's back. In her neat school uniform of dark blue with gold cuffs and collar and her regulation haircut that left only short black curls, she made the robot appear even shabbier by comparison.

If its fuel cell lasted 25,000 years, would its mind? If so, what would it do, what could it think about, sitting in a dump for 25,000 years? She couldn't even imagine that long a time. Could it shut off its mind? Was that what it meant by "dormant state"? She watched it limp along and hoped, for its own sake, that it wasn't too smart. It would get so lonely.

A red fox, made curious by the screeching sound the robot made, stepped out of the underbrush and stared, then turned tail and ran. A chipmunk sat beside a hole in a log and chirped indignantly before diving out of sight. She laughed at its quickness and its rage. No animals were allowed in the habitats; until she came to school here she'd never seen a wild one.

At the top of the rise the road crossed the route of the freight track that had once carried long trains of urban debris to the landfill. When the robot stopped here Toby said, "You turn left and go down—"

"My navigation system still functions. Do you mind if I attempt to savor my last few moments on the road?"

". . . No. But I thought—"

"You did not think. You assumed."

"You sure are grumpy for a robot!" she said and left it, walking on down the sandy track alone. Since she'd said she was going to the dump she would have to go.

Some of the squat Y-shaped concrete pylons that had held up the monorail still stood. She liked the look of the pylons against the forest background, as if they were a sculpture called "The Repeated Question" that marched down the slope and into the landfill.

Where once there had been a valley between two mountains there was now a wide and lumpy meadow. Part of one mountain had been blasted and bulldozed for soil cover. In the decades since the landfill closed, wind and weather had altered the once-smoothed surface. Fires started by lightning or spontaneous combustion smoldered and smoked until their fuel was exhausted or a downpour put them out. Where these burned spots collapsed were sinkholes, some deep enough to hold water through the driest summer. Animals drank from some of the pools and avoided others.

Scattered pines and hardwoods grew here but there were some exotic trees, born of garbage. A twisted fig survived because of the nearby ground fire that warmed its roots through the winters. A coffee tree and two orange trees bloomed each spring but never bore fruit as did the wild cherry, peach, and apple trees.

The landfill was off-limits to the students, the area judged dangerous. But the high chain-link fence that once surrounded the land had long since collapsed. Some of the students came here regularly, largely because it was for-bidden.

Toby came because she liked the dump. There was al-ways something new to see here. Odd things lay scattered about, waiting to be picked up and puzzled over. The place was full of birds, attracted by the openness, weed seeds, and berry bushes. Deer wandered through the area. Where the Academy dumped its garbage, to be graded and burned periodically, possums, raccoons, and skunks foraged. In the fall porcupines came to eat the wild apples.

She glanced back. The robot was still standing where she'd left it. It seemed to have grown shorter, settled lower on its legs. Something in its stance touched her and, without realizing it, she sighed.

Toby had a habit which sometimes made her uncom-fortable. She would try to put herself inside the skin of other people and look out from their eyes. Now she tried to imagine being this robot, seeing the world through its camera lenses, sensing as chemicals only the smells of fresh air, forest, mud, moldering leaves, and smoke. Walking on metal feet. Unfeeling. Unwanted.

The robot was a machine, but a machine that thought and spoke and sighed and showed irritation—a machine bright enough to be sent along to its own abandonment and trusted to obey that order for its own good and the good of others. Like herself.

TWO

Between her first and tenth year Toby West had lived in many places, Like her mother and grandmother, she was born in The Greenhouse, the luxury habitat in L_2 famous for its tree-lined canals. Then came the Kamar Kolony— where her memory began; Crystal City on Earth's moon; The Fountains habitat in L_3; a condominium flat on Mars; a year on location in the largest of the ringworlds then under construction; and, finally, this boarding school on Earth.

Ever since she could remember she had felt at home anywhere and nowhere. Her grandmother Lillian said change was educational, but Toby found it depressing. As soon as she'd made friends in a new place she had to move again.

Soon after she was sent to the Hillandale Academy her mother had called to say that the writers had finished a new

space saga set in the L_5 region, and she and Toby's father
and the production company were going there to film. Since
then their work had taken her parents to three other locations but they had never found the time to visit Earth.

Toby had, without being conscious of it, begun to feel
her family was little more than images on screens. When
she thought of where they might be, she imagined a habitat
orbiting at some vague place in the night sky, one more
shining light among the other unknown stars.

Sometimes, though, she dreamed of them. In one recur-
rent dream she could hear her mother's voice—that voice
that always made her think of bitter chocolate. Her mother
was not talking to Toby in the dream but to an audience,
explaining why she'd sent her only child away to school
on Earth. "I wanted her to see the blue light of snow at
dusk, to breathe the purity of mountain air, to smell real
pines and the ocean, to feel the warmth of a fireplace, to
hear the wind sigh before a rain. I wanted her to know the
reality of Earth, to know the world her people came from,
to appreciate her ancestral heritage." And then her mother
would pause and the audience would applaud and say what
a great mother she was. Toby could never see the audience,
only her father standing to one side, smiling his approval,
and Lillian was behind him, unsmiling, eyes narrowed,
counting the house. And the odd thing was that Toby could
never see where she was when watching this scene, only
that she was there but unnoticed, like a stage prop.

The longest time she'd ever spent in one place was here
at Hillandale—two years—and she had been comforted by

the idea that she had almost two years left to stay. She had counted on that time, knowing that with graduation she would have to move again to a university, probably off Earth. And after that she didn't know where she'd go. Lillian wanted her to travel for several years, visiting all the major habitats, "or perhaps the solar system—just to get the rough edges off," before joining Lillian's company, Infield Productions.

Toby didn't want to travel any farther than she had to in Space. To her, Space was a lie; what the word really meant was the emptiness between the stars, a place where people traveled only in containers, canned and vacuum-sealed against the dark and cold. And the inner space of those containers, whether they were hundred-mile-long habitats or research cruisers, was limited and confining, not grand and glorious.

Infield Productions sold that inner space with myths and dreams of Outer Space; their film fantasies helped to create the market that caused many of the new habitats to be built. If the audience believed those three-dimensional dreams playing in screens across the Terran System, to spend one's life on Earth was at best old-fashioned, at worst—a waste, or the mark of an inferior. Only in Outer Space, the stories hinted, could a person find romance, adventure, and wealth.

Perhaps because she had seen too much of the reality behind space fantasy, Earth seemed the ideal habitat to Toby. She liked living on the surface and having only sky as a roof. She enjoyed the weather everyone else complained about. She liked the sprawling, noisy cities as well as the quiet of the empty countryside. She delighted in the variety of life forms here, even the insects. The only bugs in the habitats were roaches and nobody liked them. But most of all she appreciated the security in knowing that, whatever else might happen, she could always breathe here. Nothing could shut off the life-support pumps. Nothing could puncture the sky and instantly let all the air out.

Preoccupied with her musings and the strange robot who inspired them, she didn't hear the footsteps of the small boy who climbed out of one of the gullies behind her. His school jacket was streaked with clay, his knees wet and muddy. Dirt smudged his face and crumbs of earth clung to his hair. The boy stopped, obviously startled to see her, and then, noticing her concentrated gaze, followed her line of vision. His startled exclamation made her jump.

"Thaddeus! What are you doing here?"

"Digging. What *is* that thing?"

"A robot."

"Should we hide?"

"It won't hurt us. It was sent here to junk itself."

"You *talked* to it?" he said, shocked. "A strange robot?"

"Yes."

"You're very brave. I'd never do that. You don't know if it's a rogue, or even if it was made by humans." He paused to think, then concluded, "Although I guess it must have been. They don't allow alien robots on Earth."

Before he was sent away to school on Earth, Thaddeus Hall had never seen wind or willows. When an older classmate promptly nicknamed him "Mr. Toad," and the name stuck, he was puzzled as well as highly insulted. Because he had yet to take Ancient Literature III, Thaddeus did not understand why he should be called a toad; he looked nothing like one. He was a ten-year-old with the fine bones of a child born away from Earth's gravity, blue eyes, and fair hair, and he wasn't slow and stupid as toads were reported to be but several years ahead of his age group in all his studies. His precocity, combined with his small size, made him prey to classmates with a tendency to bully.

A citizen of Earth because his parents were, Thaddeus was born aboard the merchant vessel *Alliance* en route to the Karkov Project on Andromeda's seventh planet. For the first eight years of his life that vast ship was the only world he knew. Unfortunately, having a father who was the commander and a mother who was the ship's personnel officer almost guaranteed that he did not learn that life and people could sometimes be unpleasant.

When the *Alliance* returned to Earth orbit his parents had planned to stay, retire from Space, for his sake. But in their long absence the world they'd known had changed; their family and friends were long dead, their city half its former size and unrecognizable to them. The only bright spot for them was their wealth—accumulated salaries, trusts, and inheritances had gathered interest in the time they'd been away. Most of this wealth they gave to their son, although Thaddeus had yet to fully understand this. Unable to readjust to the home world, the Halls had signed on for a research voyage to the Eridani system. They left their son behind, "for his own good." He was still recovering from their loss.

Most ex-Terran students entered Hillandale Academy at the age of five, so that their bodies could more easily adjust to and benefit from Earth's gravity. Toby had been ten years old when she arrived, and Thaddeus was nine. Both had missed those early years their classmates had had to grow, and, more important, had missed growing up with them and forming friendships and cliques. After two years at the school Toby was accepted but still considered "the new kid." Thaddeus, still grieving for the world he'd lost, was a loner.

Toby had noticed him the first day he came into her biology class. If her grandmother Lillian ever saw this boy, she'd thought, she would try to cast him in a film. He had a face one looked at, not handsome but striking, a face with character and a sense of self—qualities no acting coach or director could teach. When he saw her staring at him she smiled. Rather hesitantly he had smiled back. Some of the drama left his face then, but not the sadness. When he introduced himself and she did not so much as smile at his name, his manner relaxed. He liked her immediately, simply because she was the only student who never called him Toad.

"Why aren't you at the ball game?" Thaddeus asked now.

"I didn't feel like it."

"Me either." He looked at her more closely. "Were you crying?"

"Yes," she admitted.

"Can I ask why?"

"I have to change schools."

His reaction to that news endeared him to her forever. For a moment his eyes searched hers in stunned disbelief and then he looked as if he, too, were going to cry. He turned away quickly and his thin shoulders rose as he took a deep breath to control himself and thrust his muddy hands into his pockets. "Why do you have to go? I thought you got good grades."

"It's not grades. It's my grandmother. She's found this school on Mars some friend of hers owns and she thinks it's wonderful."

"What do your parents say?"

"Whatever she wants them to say."

"Oh. I'm sorry."

"Me, too. What were you digging for?" she said, quickly changing the subject.

"Nothing." He seemed embarrassed by the question, then volunteered, "I found some real glass bottles. But mostly I just like to dig." He glanced up at her under his long lashes to see if she was going to laugh at him. But she didn't. For children born in space the solidity of Earth had meaning and comforts that never occurred to its natives.

"Why is the robot just standing there?" he asked.

"Maybe it's trying to decide where to hide," she said. "Maybe it won't move until we go. Let's get out of sight, over there, among the trees." As they walked she told him what the robot had said.

"That's not fair," Thaddeus said when he'd heard all the story. "People shouldn't make things that can think and then send them away and abandon them when they don't want them anymore. Someone could have at least come with it to turn it off—or do *something* for it. Someone should care!"

The unexpected quaver in those last three words warned her that if she looked at him he might cry. And if he cried, he might be embarrassed and resent her, so she said casually, "That's true, Thaddeus," and stooped to pick up a plastic shard glinting in the sun. Gossip traveled fast within the walls of the Academy; having heard how he came to the school she could easily guess why the plight of the robot upset him.

The robot began to walk again. It moved across the rough terrain with awesome case, and with no trace of the limp the flat roadbed had made obvious. Several times a leg caught in a tuft of grass or a bush and the robot would stop and carefully pull itself free. When it looked small in the distance Toby began to follow.

"Can't we watch from here?" Thaddeus called after her. "It's almost out of sight."

He looked from her to the hole he'd been digging. The bottom of the hole was filling with muddy water. With a shrug he ran to catch up with her. "What if it doesn't want us to see where it goes?"

"It doesn't know we're following."

"I'd know."

"You're not a robot." She started to run; the robot had

disappeared behind some tall briars and hadn't come out again on the other side.

When they reached the briar patch the robot wasn't there. Neither was it in the gully just beyond, or in the pine grove on the rise across the gully. They hunted it for an hour or more. In their tramping about they frightened two rabbits into running, were frightened themselves by six pheasants that flushed explosively from a weed patch, and got their pants legs covered with burrs. But they found no trace of their quarry.

"Let's go back," said Thaddeus. "That robot could be all the way to the other side of the dump by now, walking around the mountain over there."

"But we'd have seen it go," she argued, but she knew he was right.

They were passing a pile of building rubble, concrete chunks and slabs so huge that they'd never been completely buried. Briars and elders grew in and around the pile. Toby walked over and sat down on a lichened cement beam. "I have to rest a minute." She reached down to pick burrs off her leg.

Thaddeus followed her but, instead of sitting, climbed up onto a slab that lay pitched at an angle, half atop another slab. He stood erect and began to walk up the slope to see how far he could get before gravity pulled him backward. He had just thrust out his arms for balance when he stopped, stared, and pointed down into the brushy tangle in the center of the pile. Pointing threw him off balance, and he flailed his arms to maintain his position but could not.

Only by jumping six feet to the ground did he avoid a nasty fall.

"It's in there!" he whispered after rubbing a painful ankle and brushing off his knees. "It's in there! Curled up like a dead spider!"

THREE

Climbing up the slab, she peered into the tangle. Thaddeus's description was apt; the robot had retracted and folded itself into a surprisingly small space. Its body lay at a slant beneath an overhang of rubble. Surrounded by brush and last year's dead leaves, only the bowl of its turret and part of the sensors gave it away.

"That's a good hiding place, but you have no view," she said. "And when it rains, water and grit from up here will wash down over you."

"Go away," said the robot.

"We will. But I think that's a boring place to spend twenty-five thousand years."

"I can see two birds' nests," said the robot.

"You're going to watch two empty nests forever?"

"One bird nest represents more evidence of life than that which exists on most of the places I have been sent to."

"Where have you been?"

"Nine planets, twenty-seven moons, and one hundred and fourteen asteroids."

She whistled softly, something her father always did when impressed. "No wonder you're old! How did you ever get back to Earth?"

"In a freight pod."

Hearing her laugh, Thaddeus decided it might be safe to get closer and he climbed up beside her. "What did you do in those places?" he asked.

"What I was sent to do. What humans could not do."

"But exactly what?"

The robot did not answer. Halfway across the landfill a robin scolded and blue jays screamed at a hawk atop a hickory snag. As the silence continued the two children exchanged a look, wondering if the robot would ever talk again. Toby glanced at her watch and saw it was past time to leave if they were to have any hope of reaching the campus before evening curfew. She was about to say so to Thaddeus when the robot spoke with startling suddenness.

"I have reviewed all relevant data. The data are incomplete. There is reference to programming done by a university. My repair record shows subsystems were replaced and modified, but gives no date. I was reprogrammed to be sent to Venus to obtain photographs and rock samples in the great polar circles. There is no record of who did that modification."

Toby interrupted. "I thought Venus was hot enough to melt lead."

"That is correct."

"Then how did you survive?"

"I contain no lead. I was next sent to the Galilean moons of Jupiter where I discovered algae in the ice of Europa. I waded sulphur lakes on Io to obtain samples of primitive bacteria. On the Uranus flight I walked on the cold moon Miranda and first heard its inner moan." The robot paused. "My performance was applauded."

"Is this true?" asked Toby, skeptical of his story.

"Robots do not lie."

"But that was done in the . . ." she had to stop and think—"about the twenty-first century?"

"Yes."

"You're four hundred years old?" The idea left Thaddeus open-mouthed with awe.

"I do not know. In Earth-time . . . that is possible. My view was limited. Aside from field tests in volcano calderas, the Arctic, and a place called Death Valley, I saw only rooms, equipment, and humans in dust-free-atmosphere garb. My data on Earth's surface is reliable only from the time I was brought back and sold."

"Why is that?" said Toby.

"My data processors were repeatedly modified and upgraded," said the robot. "Much of what humans term *memory* was dumped with each modification."

"Were all the domes still up when you got back?" asked Thaddeus, trying to prompt the robot's memory.

"Are you referring to the era when, because of human damage to the outer atmosphere, the sun's radiation nearly destroyed life on Earth and shielding was necessary over most inhabited areas, including those cities subsequently flooded when the polar ice-caps melted and the seas rose?"

". . . I guess so," said Thaddeus.

"No," said the robot, and Toby laughed.

"The domes were gone?" Thaddeus persisted in spite of being intimidated.

"Yes."

"When did they go?"

Again there was a lull, then: "According to Fatima Gilbreath's study, *Domes, Duplicity, and Why We Emigrated*, published by Quixton Press in 2348, the need for such protection ceased when the crisis had served its purpose, when Earth's population had decreased as a result of the atmospheric problem, and when five satellites had been funded, built, populated, and proven feasible for long-term inhabitation. By the end of the twenty-fourth century state scientists suddenly announced the discovery of a means of rebalancing the chemical composition of gases in Earth's atmospheric shield and proceeded to do so."

"Oh," said Thaddeus. "Would people do something like that? I mean, not fix the atmosphere if they could?"

"I know only what they did," said the robot.

"If you walked on Venus, for example," said Thaddeus, returning to that topic, "wouldn't your paint have burned off?"

"I was not painted then. The rare-book owner first committed that error."

"Did you like your owners?" Toby asked. "Do you miss them?"

What Toby called the robot's thinking lights blinked on one side, then: "I am . . ." it began. "I am an old robot." Lights rippled across its side in a jerky random sequence. "I am too old to serve as an entertainment source for two bored children who ask endless questions but believe nothing I say. I have had a long trip. I am going to rest." The robot paused, then added almost as an afterthought, "Be warned. I am equipped to defend myself against tampering or vandalism." All lights but one went off as its turret began to lower. When the turret stopped just above the ground, the last light blinked out.

"Please," Toby begged, "we didn't mean to insult you. It's just hard for us to believe you could survive all that and come back, or that you could be so old."

"You should be lecturing in schools or museums," said Thaddeus. "Those were important projects you were part of."

But neither begging nor flattery could coax the robot to speak again.

"Do you think it would shoot us if we touched it?" Thaddeus whispered as they made their way down to the ground. "I didn't see any lasers or anything like that."

"I wouldn't try. It must have something special to last this long, if what it said is true. It seems a shame to scrap it. It should have a home."

"Maybe you could talk it into coming back with us. You could keep it in your room, Toby. If it stood against the wall, it wouldn't take up much more space than a bicycle . . ." He saw her expression and shrugged. "Well, maybe a *little* more space."

"I don't think it would come, even if we asked." She didn't want to admit that she'd already thought of asking but decided not to in case the robot refused. There was the possibility that she wouldn't be allowed to keep it even if it agreed to come. All of the school's robots were utility rover units, drones to the central maintenance system, and about as interesting as mops. Besides, she wouldn't be at the school much longer.

"How about my great-grandmother?" Toby said, thinking out loud. "She's the only person I know who lives here on Earth. At a place called Fisher's Isle beside Lake Erie. Maybe she needs a robot?"

"Is that who wants you to go to Mars?"

"No. That's Lillian, my mother's mother. This is Lillian's mother, my great-grandmother. Do you think she'd want a robot?"

"I don't know," Thaddeus said politely, thoroughly confused by her relatives. "Why don't you call and ask her?"

"I don't know her," Toby admitted. "My family never talks to her."

"Why not?"

"She did something terrible to Lillian—that's what my mother said—but I don't know what it was."

"You've never seen her?"

"Just in-screen. She sent a hologram for Lillian's birthday. She's big—she was Earthborn—and she's let herself get naturally old."

"Really?" Thaddeus looked more interested. "I've never seen a *real* old person. Just pictures. Does she look scary?"

Toby shook her head. "Just her skin is wrinkled. And her hair is white." She fell silent, remembering how her mother and grandmother had reacted at seeing that hologram; they'd said how *Old World* she was; they'd looked disgusted and angry and ashamed and they couldn't stop talking about the woman—as if she had committed some crime by not remaining slender and youthful. "I kind of liked her looks . . ." Toby was talking to her mother and grandmother without realizing it. "She looked . . . strong, and comfortable. Not like . . ." She glanced sideways at Thaddeus in embarrassment, then began to jog. "Come on. We'll be late."

"If you never met her, why do you think she'd like this robot?" Thaddeus was hurrying to keep up with her longer legs.

"Because she looks *real* and so does the robot."

"Oh." He was unsure what she meant, but wasn't going to ask for an explanation. "Why do you call her Lillian and not Grandmother?"

"Because she'd have a fit if I called her Grandmother," Toby said. "*Grandmother* sounds old. And no one is old in their group. At least they pretend not to be."

He digested this in silence, then said, "I don't have any grandparents. They all died long ago, while my parents were away. I don't have any family here. Except me, of course."

The sun had set behind the clouds; night was coming early. A light mist began to fall, mixing with the haze of smoke hanging over the landfill. The wind had turned raw and both were cold in their light jackets. When they reached the road they could see the lights of the Academy against the background of the dark hills.

"Are you going to tell anyone about the robot?" Thaddeus asked.

"No," she decided after thinking it over.

"Okay. Me, too."

She gave him a grateful smile which he received with a shrug, as if loyalty were a simple gift.

The robot they had left behind stirred in its hiding place. Feet flexed and gripped the surface. Legs shifted to center the body's weight before lifting. It rose up, swaying as it balanced itself on three legs. The turret clicked as lenses adjusted for night vision and focused on the children in the distance. When trees hid the pair, it climbed out into the open, focusing its camera lenses on the spot where they disappeared.

Since the building of the huge orbiting habitats, the ease of life they offered had solved Earth's population problems. For those who remained on Earth, life anywhere but in a city had become impractical as well as unfashionable and, some said, unsafe. Most jobs were in the cities, but even workers in the farm and industrial zones commuted by air from the city to the green and brown belts. There were few small towns and villages; most of those existed solely to service recreation and tourist areas. For those ex-Terrans not frightened by so much open space and water, the Old World's ocean beaches remained popular vacation spots; some people grew mystical after spending a week beside such awesome amounts of water. Real mountains were also impressive to people born and raised in the limited spaces of the New World.

Although temperatures had returned to what was once called normal and the sea levels were dropping again, the prolonged greenhouse effect had left Earth with almost as many changes as a geologic age. Humans had come close to being the prime example of a parasite that destroys its host. During the period of increased heat and radiation thousands of species left outside the domes had become extinct. Now the only creatures that remained in the wild were those zoo and domestic animals capable of readapting and the people incapable of adapting to the cities.

Outside of the well-regulated urban centers lay the vast, deserted area called The Empty. Here were scattered groups of people who chose to make their livelihood among the ruins and new wilderness abandoned by civilization. They survived as hunters and subsistence farmers, primitive, often illiterate, their incomes supplemented by illegal means. Once they would have been called outlaws and feared; now they were called *boonies* and held in contempt.

Between the extremes of City and Empty lay the Hillandale Academy. Located in what had once been called Connecticut, the Hillandale Academy was an old and prestigious boarding school for children of ex-Terran parents. Like the aristocrats of old who sent generations of their too-young sons away to exclusive boarding schools famous for poor food, cruel social structures, cold water, and primitive sanitation—all of which were thought to be character-building deprivations—the New World's upper classes sent their children to boarding schools on Earth. Ex-Terrans felt that simply to experience the comparative isolation and hardship of living on the planet's surface would be educational and make a child more appreciative of the New World.

The Hillandale buildings sprawled over land that was once the private estate of the founder. While the wall that had served as the base of a dome had been kept up for security, all the original buildings were gone and the present ones showed signs of age. Staff and student quarters flanked an oval park over which towered the Learning Center with its old globelike solar plant. Enclosed walkways linked individual buildings and served as greenhouses as well as protection from the weather.

Begun in the days when the early habitats were still cold, geometric structures with wretched toilet facilities, chronically water-poor, and oppressively cramped and barren, Hillandale's design was intended to counteract the severe sensory deprivation of the pioneers' children. Careful attention to both color and scent had been paid to the flower gardens. Majestic old trees lined the walks and lawns. Waterfalls had been created in several creeks. There were lakes stocked with fish, in addition to fountains, reflecting pools, and three enclosed and heated swimming pools. In the New World the conspicuous consumption of water was a sign of great wealth, and the parents of these children could afford the best.

Barns and stables housed a full complement of farm animals; there were fields and orchards. The Academy, with the help of its employees and students, raised much of its own food. This was done not from need or even practicality—since little of this knowledge would be of later use—but to teach the students how and why their species had survived and evolved on their home world. This agrarian training not only gave ex-Terran offspring a sense of the physical hardship their ancestors had endured and survived, but also taught them how their own civilization began and how alien civilizations might begin, emphasizing the economy and skills that allowed the advance of technology.

Originally the farm had been a great success with students, but as generations passed and animals of any sort were barred from all colonial habitats, the concept of animals grew more and more remote to ex-Terrans. A few children still found satisfaction in harvesting and eating the foodstuffs they had helped to raise, but most found it a tiresome waste of time—or simply revolting. Each semester a few fainted on seeing where and how real milk was obtained, as well as real meat. Children born in a society where no one ever got dirty often rebelled against the work, smells, soil, sweat, and insects inherent in crude farming.

For some, Earth's insects alone explained completely why people had moved away from Earth.

Because in later life privacy might be at a premium for those students who made a career in deep space, each student had the luxury of a small but private suite. There were no shared quarters, no roommates; the Academy felt it unwise to encourage too much intimacy among the students. The ideal the administrators strived to produce were well-educated, self-sufficient individuals able to fit comfortably into any team.

By the time Toby and Thaddeus reached the campus that evening the mist had turned to rain. Both were soaking, cold, and hungry. Because running in the halls was forbidden, they took the outside route to their rooms, their need for speed outweighing their need for shelter. Toby's room was closer to the gate, and when Thaddeus did not pause at her door but called "See ya!" and raced on down the sidewalk, she grinned with the sure knowledge that he needed to go to the bathroom as urgently as she.

The lights were on and there was a fire in the fireplace when she came in. A rover unit brought the logs each morning; the computer ignited them each evening at five o'clock. The message button was blinking on her console. She barely glanced at the light as she ran to the bathroom, kicking off her muddy shoes en route. The thick brown carpet felt good beneath cold feet.

She showered and dressed for dinner. Dressing for dinner was a rule at the Academy; everyone did it, faculty and students alike, both as a relief from the school uniform and as a daily reminder that one would not always be living in the isolation of Earth's countryside. Warm again and wearing a yellow tunic shaped by a wide belt embroidered with brown abstracts, she stood drying her hair and listening to her messages.

First came a general reminder that immunization boosters against the dreaded Yardley's disease would be given Monday in the gym. Her alphabetical group was scheduled for eight o'clock, the Ws to Zs coming first for a change. She keyed her Monday wake-up call for six-thirty to give herself time for breakfast.

The next voice advised that her social studies paper, "The Ideal Habitat," had received a 10 for composition but only a 5 for attitude. "No student of Hillandale should consider Earth as an ideal habitat," the instructor's voice informed her. She made a face at the console. Then came the voice of her friend Junco, who wanted help on a physics assignment; Alex wanted to borrow one of her books; and the final voice was that of Dr. Ebert, the physician who was her Terran Guardian while she was enrolled at the Academy. Dr. Ebert invited her to breakfast in the morning. "We have a problem," the woman said.

Toby frowned as she went back to the dressing room to comb her hair. The students called Dr. Ebert "Dr. Do-we" behind her back because the woman always spoke in the plural when she talked to them. "Do we have a cold? Do we take our vitamins?" Dr. Ebert always said "We have a problem" to Toby and thought she was being clever to let her learn slowly that the problem was some failure on Toby's part alone. Toby was never at ease with the woman.

A softly insistent chime announced dinner and she looked around for the dress boots that matched her belt. From up and down the greenhouse hall came the muffled sounds of doors sliding open, voices, laughter, and the thump of feet as hungry children tried not to get caught running. At every fourth curve cameras monitored hall traffic.

Wind slapped raindrops against the transparent panels as she stepped out into the hall. Behind the plants droplets traced silver streaks on the non-glare-surface blackness. The old robot is outside in this, she thought and shivered, then reminded herself again that the robot was only a machine. And if it had walked on Venus and Io, a little rain was nothing. Still, what would it do out there alone in the dark? Or through the years to come? Could it shut off its mind at night, like a person going to sleep, perhaps set a timer for eight hours? Did robots dream?

"Did you forget something?" a passing student called, and Toby realized she was still standing in her open doorway, staring at the rain.

In bed that night she lay curled beneath her comforter, watching the dying flames behind the firescreen. Steady rain on the roof and lawns made a hissing sound that almost blotted out the gusting wind. This was one of the best things about Earth, she thought, to lie half-asleep in one's bed, watching a fire and listening to the rain. Of course it would be even better shared with a friend, but even if she had a real friend here, they'd only have to say good-bye now. How did one learn to be self-sufficient? Become a robot?

She was dreaming of night in the habitats when the shutters dimmed the solar panels to the level of late dusk. As the temperature cooled and the warm air rose, people would get out their film-flyers to ride the updrafts—soaring to the top of the habitats, where they were almost gravity-free. She could see the people gliding on their pastel winged flyers, wheeling and crying like distant gulls.

A tapping noise woke her. The clock said 3:00 A.M. Her heart was beating fast as if she'd been having a bad dream. She realized slowly that she'd been hearing the tapping in her sleep and awakened when it stopped. All she could hear now was rain.

After waiting in tense silence she stretched and turned over. An ember in the fireplace glowed like one wicked eye. Probably a broken tree branch had fallen on the roof and was rocking in the wind. Just as her eyes fell shut again there was a soft metallic click on the outer doorframe, as if someone were tampering with the identiplate. One of the older boys must be playing a trick, she thought . . . but which one would be stupid enough to be out in the pouring rain at this hour?

She was just about to tell the console to call Security when she hesitated, then said "Oval View" to clear the opaque front window. The lights around the Oval dimmed at midnight but she could still recognize her visitor by the light above her front door.

The robot stood there in the gloom, looking more like a huge bug than ever, the water dripping from its body making lines of pale light. At various places on its frame tiny colored dots glowed, lights not noticeable in daylight. With some sense of foreboding she got up and put on her robe, then reluctantly pressed the door release. Cold wet wind blew in and made her shiver.

"What are you doing here?" she whispered.

"Attempting to enter." Its voice was at low volume, as if it understood the need for stealth. "May I come in, please? I am frightened."

FOUR

"What would frighten a robot?"

Still none too awake, she stepped back to let the robot enter. Its bent leg squeaked louder than before. It stopped in the center of her study and looked much larger here than it had out-of-doors. There was a distinct smell of skunk on the wind. She shut the door and turned on the lights, then remembered to re-opaque the window.

"If you will tell me where your vac-pac may be found, I will dry myself. Barefooted humans object to wet carpets."

It sees I'm barefoot and knows what that means was her vaguely surprised thought as she said, "I don't have a vac-pac. Can you use a towel?"

"Yes. Please," came the polite reply.

"How did you find me? How did you know which door was mine?" she asked en route to the bathroom.

"My olfactory sensors are superior to those of a Batoonese dorp. I followed the scent of your footsteps."

"What's a Batoonese dorp?"

"An arboreal dorp native to Batoon."

She giggled. "Like a sloth?"

"No. Dorps more closely resemble giant spider mites. They are blind and find their prey by scent."

As she imagined such a creature her smile faded.

The robot grasped the towel with its left front foot, transferred the cloth to the right front foot, and proceeded to dry its turret, working slowly and with great care not to entangle its sensor array. It was like watching someone dry his hair with his feet, Toby thought. The three toes on each foot were jointed and as flexible as human fingers. When its lenses were polished to the robot's satisfaction it proceeded to wipe each leg, paying special attention to the joints and sockets. The towel quickly turned black.

"Another towel, please?"

She fetched a second towel and hoped that would be enough. She had only three and the laundry dispenser wouldn't give her more until tomorrow afternoon. School rules.

"What frightened you?" she asked, watching it wipe off its back using its mid-legs. "Was it a skunk?"

"Bears."

"Bears?" Robots never joked. A thrill of interested fear wiggled through her midsection. Was this why The Dump was off-limits? No one had ever warned the students about them.

"Bears," the robot repeated firmly. "My fifth owner taught me to recognize a bear when I saw one. He was a stockbroker who collected and appreciated rare old machines. When something he called The Market allowed him to leave his home, he flew his classic 23-A Bruni airtruck to remote, deserted areas. He called this Going Camping. He took me with him to share his observations of wildlife. I later confirmed and retained much of his verbal data."

The robot paused, then admitted, "I did not have visual confirmation of the bear tonight—only olfactory. I did not require more. The bear which attacked me while I was in the employ of the stockbroker stood as tall as myself when on all four feet and twice as tall when standing erect. It had a generally unfriendly demeanor, having first attacked my owner. The man instructed me to defend him. Before I succeeded in stunning the bear so we could escape, it bent my leg and broke my foot. Had I been unarmed, the bear could have easily converted me to spare parts. What are skunks?"

Fascinated with the robot's story, she had to stop and think about the skunk question. "Skunks? Oh. Small animals. Furry, black and white. Bushy tails. Pretty. But if they're frightened they spray a scent—like the smell you think is bear."

The robot had begun polishing its rear toes, looking as if it were giving itself a manicure. It paused to analyze her information and more lights blinked.

"Did you see a skunk?" she asked.

"Bears do not normally smell?"

"Not like skunk. The first bear you met must have been

sprayed by a skunk." She spoke with more confidence than she felt, since her information was based only on reading about Earth animals, but Lillian always said that if you were going to say something, to say it with authority.

"Would bears attempt to eat skunks?"

"Not if they were smart bears. The smell would make them sick—or so I've read."

"Would bears gather where I chose to hide today?"

If she said *no*, would it go back out into the rain? "They might," she said. "Maybe you'd better stay in here tonight."

"Thank you."

The tears of a great yawn blurred her view. There were still so many questions she wanted to ask but she was too sleepy to think straight. "I have to go back to bed," she said. "Make yourself at home."

"Thank you," the robot said after a thoughtful pause.

"You're welcome. Do you have a name?" she asked, then remembered that she hadn't introduced herself. "My name is Tabitha West. People call me Toby."

"Yes. Toby is what Thaddeus called you. I am called ORVIS."

"Good night, Orvis."

"Good night, Toby."

Toby drifted off to the rhythmic sound of a towel whisking over metal toes. Her last waking thought was to wonder who had given the robot such an Old World, Earth-sounding name.

When she woke the whole suite smelled of lemon. Orvis was polishing himself with her bath oil. The study floor was littered with used cotton balls, swabs, and tissues. From the looks of him he'd spent the entire night grooming. His brown finish was almost shiny, even on those spots where his paint was chipped or dented, and his chrome gleamed.

"My reflection in your mirror came as a distinct shock," he said as she stared at the mess he'd made. "I was unkempt."

"You look . . . almost new," she said politely.

"Not new. Clean. Tidy."

"You'll have to pick up that mess before the cleaning rover comes in. If it has to spend more than the scheduled time in here I get demerits. School rules."

"The rover is a maintenance drone, controlled by the housekeeping system of your central computer?"

"Yes," she said, wondering how he knew these things. "They're programmed to clean by a certain route and—"

"I understand." He closed the spout on the bath-oil bottle with a twist of two toes and with another foot began to rake the cotton and tissues into a pile. "I have selected a hiding place, if one becomes necessary. With my legs at minimum extension I will fit into your closet."

That he might remain in her room hadn't occurred to her, but of course he must, at least until dark. If he left now in broad daylight he'd attract all sorts of attention. Which might not be a good idea until she knew the rules regarding large old robots in one's room.

"Good idea," she agreed vaguely, remembering her

breakfast appointment with Dr. Ebert. "You'll have to excuse me now; I'll be late."

As she brushed her teeth she thought about the robot. It made no sense that he was afraid of bears. Not here. Maybe robots didn't lie, but this one wasn't telling the whole truth. She and Orvis were going to have a long talk when she got back.

She took the outdoor route to the dining hall, detouring around puddles on the gravel paths. The rain had stopped. Wind scudded clouds across a pale sun. Crows and blue jays called and somewhere high in a tree a squirrel was fussing. All were signs of life the warmer hall route couldn't offer.

The morning quiet was rent by the rattle and whine of the airbus lifting off from the landing field south of the administration building. On Sunday the seniors were allowed off campus. Most spent the day in the city, catching the 8:00 and 9:00 A.M. flights and returning by 6:00 P.M. at the latest. The airbus was a public transit line, linking the two nearby cities, three villages, and two schools. The bus was slow but cheap.

If the wind hadn't been so March-cold she would have stopped to watch the bus leave. She liked the antique look of them with their fat pillow shape and props on the top and sides, and she liked to ride in them. They floated along, flying so low that one could see things on the ground below and watch the shadow of the craft slide across the landscape, bending on the hills.

For her the buses more than anything else illustrated the

idea of surface atmosphere, the layer of life-giving gas trapped and held around the planet by gravity. She found the concept comforting. It was said that computers could divert or destroy any object that threatened to crash into a habitat but—because of Lillian's connections—she had seen the pictures taken when the Parkerton habitat was hit. She had seen the bodies—freeze-dried husks floating like rice spilled over the dark space—those bodies that didn't disappear in the implosion. It was worse than any fictional disaster entertainment ever made, so bad it never made the news, so bad it couldn't be borrowed from—even Lillian agreed that would be in bad taste. As she thought about those pictures she remembered Mars. Martian cities were covered by huge bubbles . . . there was no atmosphere outside. She shivered and began to run.

The lobby of the dining hall smelled of hot bread, bacon, and coffee, welcome scents on coming in from the cold. She sniffed appreciatively before hanging up her jacket and smoothing her windblown hair. Dr. Ebert always made her feel *unkempt*, as Orvis would say. She liked that word, *unkempt*.

The hall was divided into student sections and a private dining room for the teaching and administrative staff. All the rooms were formal; even the youngest children ate at white-clothed tables set for six. Regardless of how they arrived, Hillandale students left their school with table manners that would not shame them in any future human company.

At this early hour on a Sunday morning the Middle-students' dining room was almost empty, but Dr. Ebert was there waiting, seated at one of the window tables reserved for monitors and their guests. She waved and called, "Serve yourself before you join me. I'm just having Permalac."

Breakfast was Toby's favorite meal, especially on Sundays, when it was self-serve and the menu included waffles and strawberries. She decided to have a waffle first and then return for bacon, eggs, and potatoes. At the serving table she heaped a waffle high with sweetened berries and topped the mound with a blob of cream, paused to admire the colors and the smells, and then, on impulse, took a rasher of bacon to tide her over until the eggs. Adding a glass of milk and one of juice, she carried her tray to the table, being careful not to spill.

"If you keep on eating that way you'll soon catch up to your peer group, in weight if not height," Dr. Ebert observed as she watched the tray being unloaded onto the white linen surface of the table.

Unsure if the remark was meant as criticism or encouragement but determined not to let breakfast be spoiled, Toby smiled as she took her seat, thinking *humans smile to avert threat.*

Not staring at Dr. Ebert had become an effort for her ever since she'd heard Lillian say, admiringly, that the woman looked the same as when Toby's parents were students here. Dr. Ebert had been her mother's Guardian. Although it was normal for adults to avoid looking their true age, Dr. Ebert's success in that regard was remarkable. Whatever time or gravity's pull might spoil, she had corrected. Surgery, medication, and cosmetic tattooing kept her looking no more than thirty years old. Her blue eyes were perfectly shadowed and outlined, her cheeks tinted pink and tan, her lips corrected and dyed. Even her throat and hands looked young. She was slender, very blond, and immaculate in her blue dress uniform. Her manner was as careful and studied as her appearance.

Toby was never sure what was real about people like this, if anything, or if artifice so complete and perfect became its own reality—like the realness of a control computer. As one of her mother's actor friends once said, "I'm not fake anything; I'm real Sonya."

"I'm told you didn't go to the game yesterday," Dr. Ebert said, watching Toby spread strawberries evenly over the waffle.

"I went for a long walk."

"Where?"

"Along the old bike road and back."

"Alone?"

"Most of the kids went to the game."

"You should have attended. You need some team spirit."

Toby forked a bite of waffle and crushed the berries against the roof of her mouth to savor the taste. Her guardian sipped the pink silky-looking liquid that was her nourishment and watched her ward clinically.

"You're not like your parents were at your age." Her smile was intended to soften the hint of criticism. "They were both so congenial. So fun-loving. Of course," she added quickly, "you are a far better scholar than either, but you could be popular, too—if you made a little effort."

Toby thought that over. It was true; she wasn't much good at friendships, but she thought it was because she'd never had the time in one place to make them last. She wasn't sure she wanted to be *popular*. She couldn't quite imagine her mother and father as children but she knew they were still popular. They were always surrounded by people: actors, writers, set designers, technical people from the studio. And all of them, her parents, their friends, and even Lillian, were Talkers. When she still lived at home sometimes people would talk to her for hours on end and she never had to say much because they didn't want to listen to her. She'd always associated being popular with talking too much.

On those rare days between films, when there was no work or guests, her parents hadn't talked much to each other. They had talked to her, competing for her time. They laughingly called this "Prime Time for Toby" and said she was their "Number-One Audience." As their audience she was attentive and appreciative of their attention. Sometimes she was even interested in what they told her. But what she remembered most was that sometimes, when they had been talking to her for an hour or more, they would stop and say, "So what's new with you?" and she could never think of the correct answer. Or at least not anything important enough to tell them. Being with popular people was exhausting.

Becoming aware that the silence had lasted too long, she glanced up to see Dr. Ebert watching her. "Is that my problem?" said Toby. "That I'm not more popular? Is that why they want me to change schools?"

"No. Oh, no. But, as I was saying, building a support network among members of one's peer group can't start too early. School prepares one for adult life. The people you meet now will someday be scattered around the entire System. You never know when you'll come in contact with them again and old friendships often prove useful . . ." She broke off. "Yes. Well. What we wanted to discuss. Your mother called back yesterday afternoon."

"I never got the message."

"She called me. She was upset because you were so unenthusiastic about the new school. She believes, and your grandmother apparently agrees, that the new school would be more suitable for you. It's in the new blister settlement with a wonderful view of the canyon—"

"I've been to Mars," Toby interrupted. "I hated it. It's dead . . . and the wind blows sand against the bubbles so that you always hear that hissing sound."

"But that's an incidental. Your mother is *so* enthused about the school. It specializes in the communication arts. Its founder is apparently a friend of your family's. An expert in media. They offer . . ."

They were getting Dr. Do-we on their side? To try to talk her into wanting to go, so that if she hated it there they would say it wasn't all their decision? Breakfast began to sour in her stomach.

"And you can visit the school on spring break instead of going to the shore," Dr. Ebert was saying. "If you like it there and wish to transfer, I'd make arrangements to ship your personal things. We would be sorry to see you leave Hillandale, but if it means your receiving a more relevant education . . ." The expression on Toby's face made her pause.

"You must be realistic, Tabitha. Your parents want this for your own good. No matter how much you enjoy it here, it is doubtful that you will ever make a career of research in any form, and that is what the Academy best prepares its students for. Your studio is family-owned and you will become a part of it, eventually head it in all probability. And in that capacity you can do so much more for humankind than you ever could elsewhere." She waited for a response from Toby and on getting none sighed and said, "I'm sorry, my dear, but nothing lasts forever."

With a near-panic feeling that doors of choice into her future were slamming shut, Toby managed to speak calmly. "I don't want to go to school on Mars. I don't want to go anyplace. I don't want to make pictures. I don't want to worry about the first month's gross. I don't want to spend my life talking to actors. I want to stay here, on Earth."

"Doing what?"

"I don't know yet. Why do I have to decide at twelve what I want to be for the rest of my life? Would two years from now be too late? Or even five years from now?"

"No. But the fact remains that you are not yet independent." Dr. Ebert paused to let this unpleasant fact sink in. "While it is gratifying to hear how much you like Earth, I'm afraid flight reservations have been made for you to visit the new school. You're obviously not happy about this, but I must point out, Tabitha, that it's not as if you were an infant. In two years, when you leave the Academy—or perhaps this new school—you will be going on to a university. After that you will begin your career. That's not so many years away, although the time probably seems long to you now."

"What you're saying is that I don't have any choice, that I shall do and be what my family orders?"

The woman opened her mouth to reply, then thought better of what she was about to say. "No. Not necessarily. Perhaps you should discuss this with your parents at greater length. It might be wise for you to call them."

"Are they still on location?"

"I'm sure their studio office could tell you."

Toby saw Dr. Ebert looking at her as if she were feeling sorry for her; since Toby was feeling rather sorry for herself at the moment, she decided she'd better change the subject.

"Are there school rules against students having robots?"

"None that I know of. Why?" The woman seemed startled by the question.

"I was thinking of getting a robot."

"A toy? A pet? Something furry?"

"No. A real robot. A big one."

"For what purpose?"

"Multi-purpose."

"Oh? Well. In the past, several students developed quite clever specialized robots as part of their university admissions projects. Was that what you had in mind?"

"Something like that."

Dr. Ebert nodded approval. "Robots are expensive, but we might find something suitable. If you decide to stay here at the Academy. A good used model? Perhaps a kit you could build yourself? Yes, I think that might be an excellent project."

Toby noticed Dr. Ebert seemed relieved to talk about robots rather than personal things, but then she was the Guardian of at least ten other students and responsible for everything from seeing that the children stayed healthy and weren't taken advantage of, to making sure they didn't exceed their allowances. It couldn't be an easy job, being a substitute parent. And if a Guardian liked a student, the student would just graduate and go away and the Guardian would probably never see him or her again. No . . . being a Guardian wouldn't be an easy job. Maybe Dr. Do-we wasn't the world's brightest person, but she tried to be kind in her own way. Maybe she didn't like getting up early on a Sunday morning to have breakfast with a student and do what parents should have done, only to be resented for her efforts.

"I'm sorry to be angry," Toby apologized. "It's my problem and not your fault, whatever happens. Thank you for taking the time to see me instead of just calling. I appreciate it."

"You're—uh—welcome." The woman seemed surprised to be thanked. "It's all part of the job—uh, the pleasure of working with young people, watching them mature—as you are doing. We try to do our best."

FIVE

Orvis was watching an entertainment channel when she got back to her rooms. Horrible slimy creatures the color of a nasty bruise were oozing over the pink sands of an alien world, apparently in pursuit of the humans fleeing before them. She thought she recognized one of her parents' pictures. Quality stuff, as her father laughingly termed it.

"Totally impossible," was the robot's greeting. "Unless those organisms could ingest and metabolize replacement nutrients, the loss of such a disproportionate amount of their body fluids through slime lost to the sand would result in death within minutes. To say nothing of tissue abrasion. And the remote chance that they would be interested in eating foreign protein or so much as recognize humans as a possible food source. The—"

"It's just for fun, Orvis. To entertain. Not to think about."

"But the plot is inconsistent, the whole situation implausible. All worlds conform to a set of inherent natural laws. Those life forms could not exist in that environment . . ."

"I guess robots have trouble appreciating fantasy," said Toby.

There was a short silence while Orvis considered that. "My definitions of the word *fantasy* do not include *stupidity*," he announced.

"There are no school rules against students having robots," she said to change the subject. "You don't have to hide in my closet."

"That is good news." His comment, so humanly gracious yet totally lacking the inflection of enthusiasm a human would have given the remark, made her laugh, but Orvis went right on. "In order to enter the space of the closet I would have had to tilt my frame sixty-two degrees left while simultaneously telescoping my left legs down and my right legs up and turning as I tilt. I would have found such movement awkward when new. In my present condition the result might have been mechanical break-down and entrapment."

"Orvis? I've been thinking. I don't believe you came here last night because you were afraid of bears."

"You don't believe a robot?"

"No. Why did you come? At the dump you didn't even like me. Or Thaddeus. Or you didn't seem to." When he didn't answer she sighed and sat down in her armchair. Having him around was like having a moody roommate.

Moody people always made her feel self-conscious. But a moody robot?

In-screen purple monsters oozed into a fantastic ship while humans fled screaming, shooting lasers and hitting nothing. With half her mind on the film she mulled over her situation: My parents were five when they came here to school. Just babies. Mother said Lillian came to see her twice in the first four years, which was two times more than they've come to see me. "We see each other when we call, darling. What real purpose would an actual trip serve? I'd lose at least ten days in travel time." That was true, of course.

"You caused me to think." Orvis's voice jarred her from introspection. "You asked if I always did what I was told to do. Yes. I was created to obey. Until you questioned me I had never thought of not obeying. After you and Thaddeus went away, I began to think. Logic suggested that there was no reason for me to remain inactive until I cease to function. I had obeyed my last direct command by reaching the landfill. Thus, I was free.

"Coming here last night was my first act of independence. It was disorienting. I could not think of another destination. My second act of freedom was to clean myself without being ordered to do so. The third was turning on your vu-screen in an attempt to improve my mind." He turned off the screen. "One liberty leads to another, one choice to another, until self-discipline must be imposed to avoid mental chaos. Freedom is frightening. There are no established boundaries."

It was her turn to think. What did a robot do if it didn't follow orders? Over a long period of time? What if it decided to do something bad, or at least socially unacceptable?

"Aren't you ever going back to the dump?"

"Yes. At 8:04 this evening a satellite will signal to me at those coordinates. I will acknowledge. The satellite will then signal the Federal Android/Robot Directory to note that I am at my assigned final destination. By 8:06 my FARD file will be archived. By 8:10 P.M. I shall be on my way out of the landfill. I am going to travel and study birds. I shall keep to unpopulated areas; avoiding humans. I may be able to walk over much of this planet's surface before wearing out."

"No one will mind if you travel?"

"No. No one is responsible for me. I have no owner. I estimate 92.8 percent of all humans will not willingly assume responsibility for anything they do not have to assume responsibility for."

"I never heard of a *free* robot." She wasn't sure it was allowed.

The front door sang its three-note song before she could finish the thought. Preoccupied, she opened the door to find Dr. Ebert there, holding a printout.

"We thought you might like to look at robots in the various supply catalogues. These are the access codes that you will . . . that you could . . ." The woman's voice faded away and her eyes widened as she got a good look at Orvis. ". . . Uh, you could . . . What *is* that?"

"A robot."

"A robot?"

"An old model."

"Oh." The woman stepped back but kept her hand on the doorframe. "May I ask where it came from and how you got it into your suite without being seen?"

Toby considered telling a lie, but once a lie was told, you usually had to tell more, and then remember each one. She'd never been good at remembering lies, and so she told the truth. Or nearly so. "We met on the old bike road yesterday. It was going to the dump. It's been scrapped."

"It was alone?"

"Yes."

"And you brought it back with you?"

"Don't you think it's interesting? I do."

"Oh . . . yes. I've never seen anything quite like it. But it's not the sort of thing you should have. For one thing, it's too large. For another, other than in pictures . . . Do you know what it was designed to do?"

"No." That wasn't quite true but sometimes the less one told grown-ups, the better off one was. "It talks," she volunteered. "Its name is Orvis."

"Really?" Dr. Ebert was making an effort to be understanding. "Do you think it would speak to me?"

"You can try" Toby sincerely hoped Orvis was smart enough not to talk too much.

"Robot?" Dr. Ebert sounded as if she were talking to a drugged patient. "Can you tell us what work you were designed to do?"

"I am a multi-purpose unit."

"What a primitive speaker. It's almost frighteningly impersonal!"

From the lawn outside a boy shouted to a friend, "Hey, Worm-breath? Wait up! Race you to breakfast!"

The doctor glanced around, then with the air of a conspirator came in and shut the door. "Robot? What specific functions can you perform?"

"I am a multi-purpose unit."

"It's very old," Toby said to fill the awkward silence.

"Is Orvis your name or an acronym?" Dr. Ebert asked. She spoke rather loudly, as if Orvis were deaf.

"An acronym."

"What does it stand for?"

"I do not remember."

"For whom were you designed?"

"I do not remember."

"Why don't you remember?"

"Part of my early data were deleted for security purposes."

"You were a military unit?"

"I am a multi-purpose robot."

"Are you *deliberately* being evasive?"

"Yes."

He's talking too much, thought Toby; he's going to get in trouble.

"It must have been quite an advanced machine for its time." No emotion showed on Dr. Ebert's flawless face as she handed Toby the sheet of paper that was the reason for her visit. "As the person responsible for your welfare here, Tabitha, I'm afraid we must insist that this machine be scrapped as originally planned. It is nothing to play with and, old as it is, might be extremely dangerous."

"Orvis isn't dangerous."

"You have no way of knowing that. I'm afraid I must enforce my legal authority—the robot goes to the landfill. Take it to the road and order it to follow its original programming. The sooner the better. Is that understood?" When Toby reluctantly nodded, Dr. Ebert opened the door to leave, then paused to ask. "Did you place the call to your mother?"

"No. It wouldn't make any difference. She'd just say the same thing."

"Still, we might try." The woman gave her a bright false smile. "I'll check back with you in an hour to see that this thing is gone."

No sooner had the door shut behind her than Orvis said, " 'The common wild pigeon, or stock dove, is a bird of passage.' Gilbert White, *The Natural History of Selborne*, 1788." He paused for less than a second and added, " 'But where in my memory do You abide, Lord?' Saint Augustine, 354–430."

Toby stared at him. "What are you saying?"

"Quotations. I am running a random check to determine if my memory and intelligence are still intact. In the past twenty-four days only yourself and Thaddeus have spoken to me as an intelligent entity. All others addressed me as that person just did. If all but yourselves spoke to me in the same manner, then why? It occurred to me that I had suffered brain damage which was unapparent to myself-but obvious to others."

A series of tiny multi-colored lights flickered under his turret and up and down his sides; from his speakers came a babble of voices, bits of music, formulas, sounds she couldn't identify. It was like listening to a radio on seek-command. "My memory is intact," he announced and the lights and sounds ceased.

"Who is Saint Augustine?"

"An ancient mind who also questioned the reliability of information in his data banks."

"Why would that stuff be in your memory?"

"My fourth owner was a rare-book dealer. He was ignorant of robots and assumed I could do anything. After talking with me for several days he said a civilized mind should contain more than technical data. He took me to his warehouse where there were seventeen unkempt aisles of old books and directed me to read, sort, catalogue, and reshelve the lot. He said there was a printer in his office and I was to run ten copies of the inventory list when I was finished. As a result I would then be programmed to help him find books should a customer wish to make a purchase."

"What did you say?" The task seemed overwhelming to Toby.

"Yes."

She grinned. "How long did it take you?"

"Two months. His desire to talk delayed me. He repeatedly asked what I had learned. Answering took longer than shelving. I found nontechnical writing confusing, illogical, and often in error. It required my full capacity to absorb. As a by-product I updated my vocabulary in six languages. When I was through, my owner created a routine whereby I joined him in his rooms at the end of his workday when he would give me more books to scan. He called this Spending-the-Evenings-Together-Reading."

The words evoked an image of a white-haired man and the old robot in a cozy book-lined room. Orvis would have to scan a book only once to retain it in its entirety, but did he truly understand what he read? "What all did you learn?"

"Shall I repeat that total data input period?"

"No!" Could a robot be sarcastic? "Just tell me one thing you wouldn't have known or thought about otherwise. If you didn't read with that man."

"Humans believe they have a soul and non-humans do not."

"I always thought everything had a soul—including robots."

"Soul is not listed in my Parts and Systems Indices. There is no repair schematic for such an item. Also, soul is not shown on any chart of human anatomy."

"Soul isn't a thing you can see."

"Please define the term."

"It's . . . It makes you what *you* are—someone or something different from anything or anyone else. Unique."

"Like a registration number?"

"No. That's just to identify you if you're lost or stolen.

Your soul is . . . personality, energy, what your parts and experience make you. Your own spirit—and don't ask what spirit is. I can't define that either."

"When I cease to function, will my undefinable soul go to that uncharted region of the sky known as Heaven?"

"You read about that, too?" Toby wished she could change the subject, being quite out of her depth. "I imagine your energy goes back into the universe, but I'll have to think about it. Is that where you learned about birds? In the old books?"

"No. The old books are obsolete; many of the species listed have long been extinct. Eighty-two percent of my data on birds was gained by scanning books; the balance was gained by observation in the field and from my last owner, an ex-space captain who was interested in flight. Not space flight but winged flight. He said he wished to soar upon the winds. He admired birds."

Thaddeus arrived then, out of breath from running. "I knew it!" he said, pointing to Orvis as she opened the door. "I knew she was talking about our robot! I was on the other side of the hedge and heard her tell the dean 'huge insect' and 'too intelligent,' so I tiptoed closer to listen. She's really upset, Toby. She said the authorities should come and dispose of it and—" At that Orvis made a noise and Thaddeus apologized. "I'm sorry but that's what she said."

"What did Dr. Milhaus say?"

"He said he wanted to check something and then he'd come and see for himself. I ran ahead to warn you. How'd you get the robot to come here?"

"His name is Orvis," she said, and told him the bear story.

"Are there bears?"

"I don't know."

"Does Dr. Ebert know he came here by himself?"

"No. She thinks I brought him."

"Good. Otherwise she'd really be scared."

"Shall I hide in the closet?" said Orvis.

"I think it's too late for that." Through the window Toby could see the dean and Dr. Ebert coming across the lawn. By the time the chime rang, her stomach hurt.

Dr. Milhaus, the dean, was an ex-Terran like his students. To account for his unusual height and slenderness, student myth had it that he was born on a hi-grav world and the trip to Earth had so disoriented him that he could never stop growing. He was a sober, austere man beginning to show his age in spite of youth treatments. His manner with the students was one of respect, so long as they accorded himself, the Academy, and the Academy's rules similar respect.

"I wonder if I might see that robot?" was his greeting. Only after receiving Toby's permission did he step inside. "Oh, my!" he murmured. "It is, isn't it?"

She was going to ask "Is what?" but after glancing from his face to that of her Guardian, she decided to be quiet. Dr. Milhaus needed sun; he'd gotten awfully pale over the winter. And he was shaking a little, too. Maybe he was sick. When he saw her staring at his trembling hands he quickly put them in his pockets.

"Admittedly this is very . . . interesting, Miss West. I can readily understand why you wanted to salvage this unit. At your age I would have, too." He attempted an understanding smile that somehow failed. "Your Guardian was correct in saying that students were allowed to own robots. However, that rule excludes hazard or military types. This robot seems to be both."

"You are in error," said Orvis.

The dean ignored him. "I will check with the regional authorities as to who is responsible for this robot, but for now, Miss West, I want it to go immediately to the landfill. Arrangements have been made to clear the campus. We are fortunate that it's Sunday and most of the students sleep in . . ."

"But Orvis isn't dangerous," said Toby. "He's a little grumpy, but—"

"No arguments. It must go. Now!"

From the expression on the man's face Toby saw that begging wouldn't be wise. She sighed and turned to Orvis. "I'm sorry. You have to go."

"Yes," said Orvis.

"To the landfill," insisted the dean.

"Yes." Orvis headed toward the door, and the dean and Dr. Ebert quickly moved away. The call light on Toby's monitor began to blink and the dean answered, "Milhaus here." The caller was one of the security staff.

"They're all inside, sir, except for two boys down by the trout ponds where there's no loudspeaker. They can't see the campus from there."

"Good. The robot is coming out now. Keep it under close surveillance and let me know where it goes."

Before her Guardian could stop her, Toby ducked past Dr. Ebert and followed the robot outside. Thaddeus followed her. The security aircar appeared from over the barns and hovered nearby.

"Are you going to hide in the same place?" she asked the robot.

"If I told you I would not be hidden."

"If you get tired of traveling and want a place to stay, I have a great-grandmother here on Earth. On Fisher's Isle. On Lake Erie. Maybe you could go there?"

"Where's he going?" Thaddeus wanted to know.

"I'll explain later." She tilted her head toward the security guards watching their approach to the gatehouse.

They walked Orvis through the gate and down the drive to the old road, then watched him turn north, toward the landfill. If he answered their "Good-bye, Orvis" they couldn't hear; the aircar was coming closer and its hum muffled other sounds. They glanced up at it just for a moment and when they looked again for Orvis he had disappeared.

SIX

Blended right into the pines." The guard at the gatehouse was on the intercom as they walked back. "Yessur. We'll find it. Yessur. We'll keep everyone inside until we do."

"They'll never see that robot again," Thaddeus predicted. "He's too smart to get caught."

"We won't either." The thought made her sad. By eight o'clock tonight, while she was supposed to be studying, Orvis would begin his trip. His data probably included all sorts of maps, but would maps be enough? Was he used to walking alone in the dark? Of course he was, she told himself.

The dean came to meet them as they walked back across the Oval. "Did you see which way it went?" he asked. They shook their heads. "You're sure?" They nodded. After staring at them for too long he decided to appeal to them as equals.

"You would have no way of knowing this at your age," he said, "but that robot is extraordinarily old. You can tell by its crude, utilitarian design. The library computer tells me that ORVIS robots were initially top secret, built in university labs with military funding. The name is an acronym for Overland Reconnaissance Vehicle In Space. The ORVIS robots were some of the earlier deep-space research types used to explore planets and asteroids within our solar system. To collect botanical and geological specimens, photographs. That sort of thing. Later, they were sent to Andromeda and beyond. Apparently some returned. I'll know more about it after I hear from the federal authorities, of course. But to get back to you two, it was foolhardy of you to be alone with it, to bring it to campus without asking some responsible adult's permission."

"Do you *really* think it's dangerous?" Toby couldn't believe that.

"Very much so! It seems to be a variation of the discriminating models—discriminating meaning they could, within reason, think for themselves when working under conditions where contact with their ship was impossible. Their data processors were far in advance of their time. They were fitted with electronic nerve nets. Some were made self-educating—the rationale being that the robots could tap into certain computers and modify their data as it became necessary. They could read, analyze, interpret . . . Their cumulative intelligence potential was extraordinary. Stupid idea, really! Ivory-tower stuff. Made them overqualified for their work, temperamental, and extremely dangerous. Just because you can create such a thing is no excuse for doing so!" The very idea seemed to anger him.

"People are like that," said Toby. "Why does that make Orvis dangerous?"

Light gleamed off the ridge of Dr. Milhaus's sharp nose as he glanced down at her. "Because, Miss West, the thing is a *robot*. Not a person. And you don't know where it's been or what terrible things it may have learned in four hundred years. Think, girl! A robot with a mind of its own—so to speak—is capable of ignoring instructions, of disobeying. If it turned on you, you'd be helpless against it. History records that several of those early units refused to return to their research ships, choosing freedom on uninhabitable worlds rather than following commands. One was forcibly brought back. It attacked the ship's officers and killed several before it could be jettisoned. The units were armed to defend crews if attacked by alien life forms. And, of course, the fuel cell makes firing on them out of the question. Unlike humans, they were made almost immortal." He seemed to brighten then, concluding, "But this one won't bother anyone now."

"No," Toby agreed, then wondered why Dr. Milhaus was suddenly convinced of that.

At 8:00 P.M. she got up from her desk and went out into the center of the Oval to stare up at the sky, hoping to see one tiny, swiftly moving "star," the satellite that was supposed to signal to Orvis. The sky was clear; even with the Academy's lights she could see thousands of stars overhead. By concentrating she counted five lights moving too fast to be true stars; three had the telltale fuzzy glow of habitats and the other two were so bright that she was almost sure they were space ships docked in Earth's orbit, their hulls reflecting the light of tomorrow's sun.

A glance at her watch brought a distinct sense of loss; the blue numbers said 08:14.36. Not only had she missed seeing the satellite, but by this time the old robot would have left the landfill. "Good-bye, Orvis," she whispered. "Have a good time. See lots of birds. And don't get caught." And then she felt silly. The robot wouldn't care if she wished him well, or anything else. Still . . . he had come to see her.

As she walked back to her door she could hear the sound of the bulldozer from the direction of the dump, the metallic squeal and clank of its treads clear in the still night. It seemed an odd time to be burying garbage.

When her studies were finished, on a whim, she asked the computer for the Academy's family-background section of her personal file. To her surprise, she got it. Listed there were the names, occupations, last-known addresses, and contact codes of her family for six generations on both sides—five generations of whom had sent at least one student to Hillandale. There was a genealogy chart so large it had to be viewed in sections. Most of the names meant nothing to her, but when she finally found her grandmother's name she was shocked to see that Lillian had two younger brothers. Both had wives, children, and grandchildren . . . cousins her own age! She grinned at the idea, wondering where they lived and what they looked like and if they knew about her. Why hadn't Lillian ever mentioned them? How wonderful! And lucky . . . the rules on how many babies you could have must be different here. But maybe they were as poor as her great-grandmother? Lillian always said how poor she was and what an awful place she lived in and how the old woman was too stubborn to know any better.

Scanning up from Lillian's name she came to her great-grandparents: James Wendell Philips (2402–2541) and Mary Moorehouse Philips (2425–). Under their names, in brackets, their residence was listed as: Earth, Fisher's Isle, Southern Shore of Lake Erie, North American Continent. Later in the file she found a map. Fisher's Isle was no longer an island but a wide peninsula jutting into the lake. Somehow that fact made both her great-grandmother and the woman's home seem more real.

She asked the computer for copies of the genealogy chart and the map and went to bed to study the printouts and wonder what the place was really like. She'd never been in a private home on Earth. She wished there were a way to meet her great-grandmother before leaving. But Lillian would never approve of that, and therefore her parents wouldn't allow it.

A yawn made her eyes water as she mulled over what the dean had said about other robots like Orvis, robots who ran away rather than go back to their ships and servitude. What was the difference between a robot as smart as Orvis and a slave? Slaves ran away. But then robots didn't have to eat or sleep, or worry about weather. Running away might be easy for them. If she ran away to escape going to Mars . . .

Since the Academy was so isolated, walking away as Orvis planned to do would only get a person lost. To take the airbus she would need a boarding pass—which the pilot matched against the passenger list on his screen. Probably the easiest way to go would be to borrow one of the staff's aircars. Two boys had done that the year before and had been expelled. If she got expelled, that would guarantee her going to Mars . . . but she *might* get as far as her great-grandmother's place before the authorities caught up with her. Knowing she'd never have the nerve to steal anyone's car, she sighed and fell asleep.

What with one thing and another Toby didn't see Thaddeus all week. With vacation time so close both had exams to study for, essays and reports to finish. All students were confined to campus until Wednesday; the explanation given by the Academy was the report of a rabid dog in the area.

In biology she finished work on her lab paper, "The Clotting Process," and dictated the copy to the printer. From the windows of the lab high in the Learning Center one could see the landfill sloping up to join the mountains, the smoke a mist above the trees. Each time she glanced that way she thought of Orvis and wondered where he was and if he was enjoying his travels.

In her evening dairy class she learned how to make cottage cheese, but not why the stuff was called that. She'd never liked it and knowing how it was made did not alter her opinion. But she did enjoy leaving the dairy and wandering back through the barns, seeing the cattle bedded down for the night, smelling their scents. They watched her with their great dark eyes and did not protest when she patted their furry foreheads. She would miss real animals; there were none off-Earth. Only furry robots. Unless she attended a Terran college she wouldn't see real animals for years. Two weeks more before spring break, before leaving. And she still hadn't told anyone but Thaddeus about it. She wasn't sure why—except maybe that she was afraid she would start to cry.

On Friday a freight container came for her, a gift from her parents. Inside was expensive clothing suitable only for the tropics of Earth or the warmth of a Martian blister colony. There was also an assortment of exotic food in cans. The sight of the box made her angry and she promptly gave it all away, much to Dr. Ebert's disapproval. "Your parents meant that as a treat for you, dear. They'd be so hurt if they knew."

"Don't worry," said Toby, who recognized a bribe when she saw one, "they'll never think about it again."

On Saturday she was up at dawn and put on her gray exercise suit, dressing for drabness. She was going to run to the landfill before breakfast, to see if she could trace Orvis's route out of the area. Early as it was, a few other people were out jogging around the Oval track or doing their warm-ups. She trailed two instructors out the gate and down to the old road.

Morning fog softened the outlines of the greening hills.

An unusual number of birds were singing, although she could see only crows and several flocks of geese flying over in straggly formations. Deer were feeding among the pines, unbothered by the joggers. She saw no bears, but ten minutes down the road came upon Thaddeus leaning against a white oak, hands shoved into his muff-pocket, looking small and lonesome. At the sound of her footsteps he stiffened, then, seeing who it was, grinned, and took off at a jog.

"I was sort of hoping you'd come along," he said when she caught up. "You want to go see if we can track the robot?"

She grinned with pleasure to see he'd had the same idea.

They stopped to rest at the top of the slope where the Y-shaped pylons marched off to the landfill. The sun had come up and Toby was sweating in spite of the cool air. She wiped her face on the back of her sleeves and let her heart slow down. Two years and she still wasn't used to this gravity, she thought impatiently.

Then suddenly she was off again, running down the slope, dodging wet bushes, jumping over logs and stones as if chased by wild things.

"Hey, wait up!" Thaddeus called, half scared. "What's wrong?"

She didn't have the breath to spare to tell him she'd seen tire and tread marks where only animals had walked the week before. Ahead, between the brush and pines, were glimpses of earth scraped raw by a bulldozer. The stretches of exposed clay were slick and shiny, as if the blade had scraped them at high speed. She stopped to look more closely; thick roots were sheared clean.

"It looks as if they chased him with the blade down." Thaddeus caught up, panting, to give words to her fear.

"He said he could defend himself."

"Sure. But what would happen to him if he tried?" Thaddeus kicked at a clod of dirt. "You know people don't let robots get away with shooting at them. I think they buried him up here."

"They wouldn't do that! He's alive! He's got a mind!"

"He's just dangerous junk to them."

"But he could run. He could get away . . ." She could tell by his expression that Thaddeus wasn't counting much on that chance.

"If he'd got away, the dean would have come to ask us more questions about him, to find out if we knew where he went," he said.

"Maybe." She wasn't going to admit that and, without waiting for the pessimistic Thaddeus to follow, she set off, inspecting each pile of dirt, every pit and hole she came to, any place large enough to hide a robot his size. As she went she called, "Orvis? Where are you, Orvis?," but softly, for fear her voice would carry in the stillness to the runners up on the road. If Orvis truly had the hearing of a Batoonese dorp, he would answer her. If he still could.

But there was no answer.

Thaddeus watched her with a quizzical look on his foxbright face. Slowly his expression changed to musing and what could have been envy. He kicked a stone, then another, then shrugged and at last set off on his own, hunting and calling for the robot.

Noon found them together again on the far northern edge of the field where the landfill ended and the mountain began. A rude moat, deep and wide at the mountain base, had been left around the landfill to trap eroding soil. The place was a jumble of rocks, boulders, shrubs, and gullies. The bulldozer had been all over the area, repeatedly.

"Orvis?" Toby climbed up on a rock. "Orvis? Answer me? Please?"

"If he's buried here we'll never get him out," Thaddeus predicted glumly. "Not even with dynamite. We could dig for years and not move this stuff."

"But we haven't found any of his tracks."

"The bulldozer probably scraped them all away—just in case you came looking."

"Maybe they chased him here and he ran up the mountainside?" she said, still hoping. But by now, tired from the morning's efforts and missing breakfast and lunch, she didn't believe herself anymore. It wasn't fair. The robot wasn't going to hurt anybody. Why couldn't they have let the poor thing alone? And the worst thing was, if something bad had happened to him, it was probably her fault. He wouldn't be in this situation if only she hadn't first spoken to him.

"Toby!" Thaddeus's whisper made her shiver. "That rock is *moving*." He was pointing at a slab of granite larger than her bathroom. As she looked, one end of the stone dropped down, rasping against other stones as it subsided. The movement was repeated and each time the scraping was louder. A small avalanche of stones rattled down into the moat, thudding and rolling around the trees reaching up from the trench.

"Orvis? Is that you?" She went to take a closer look and Thaddeus caught her arm.

"Don't," he begged. "What if it's a bear?"

"You and Orvis and your bears!" she said in disgust. "A bear would be dead under all that weight." She pulled free, not seeing Thaddeus's chagrin. "Orvis? If that's you, keep trying!" She looked around, searching for a sturdy branch to use as a lever, thinking that she and Thaddeus could help pry up the stone.

"It *is* him!" As Thaddeus spoke there was a scraping sound that set her teeth on edge. The stone tilted at an angle and one of the robot's feet reached out from under the pile. The toes anchored on a large piece of granite, tightened, and the leg contracted. A second foot appeared and the slab was nudged repeatedly. With scraping and scratching Orvis climbed slowly up out of the hole. Dirt and pebbles dribbled from his back.

"Why have you been calling me?"

"We were worried about you," she said.

"How long have you been under there?" asked Thaddeus.

"Six days."

"Ever since you left? Why? You could get out."

"Why should I come out? I have been judged obsolete and useless. I have been judged dangerous and stupid. Logic suggests that if my independent status is so great a threat to humans that they attempt to maim and bury me without discussion and without deactivating my brain, there is little point in my exploring a world dominated by such creatures. My appearance would repeatedly inspire attacks and attempts to destroy me. Therefore, when I was bumped and pushed into this depression between the stones, I simply remained where I fell while the machine pushed more rocks over me."

"How could you let them do that to you?" Toby said.

"I could not leave the area before acknowledging the satellite signal. The aircar and bulldozer operator were persistent. I was pursued from one side of the area to the other. When the satellite passed overhead I had time only for a rudimentary response. Now the Registry computer will show that my reply was only a fragment and conclude that I am brain-damaged as well as junked."

"But when the men had gone, why didn't you at least dig out and go where you could see something?" Toby persisted.

"For what purpose?"

"It beats being buried!"

"Have you ever been buried?"

"No . . . ," she admitted.

"Extreme pressure combined with total lack of light does something to the mind. Like a Venusian storm. Forty-six percent of my brain is devoted to sight and analysis of what is seen. Without light the other sensory units are unbalanced. I had almost ceased all thought by the time I heard your voice. Why did you call me?"

"I was worried about you," she said again.

Orvis thought this over. Rows of lights blinked. "I have referenced both thesaurus and dictionary data. Do you feel responsibility for my welfare?"

"No," she said too quickly, not wanting to admit to feeling where a robot was concerned. She took refuge in Thaddeus's cry. "But someone should care."

Orvis thought again. "Are you defining *care* in the sense of guardianship or in the sense of human affection and or attachment?"

"Both, I guess," she admitted with a sigh.

"Do you then care about this unit?"

"I must or I wouldn't be out here."

"Logic would suggest that your understanding of the word *care* would include some degree of *responsibility*. Why should you feel responsible for what happens to me?"

"Because." Toby sighed, then continued, "it's not your fault you're here. Or that you're in the shape you're in. Somebody made you. Gave you a mind. That makes you alive."

"Artificial intelligence is not life," said Orvis. "Knowing that I know does not make me alive, merely sentient. And that is debatable."

"Don't argue."

"I am stating fact. What plans do you have for me?"

She had none but this was no time to admit it.

When she did not answer Orvis said, "If you bothered to find me and call me back, you must have had some logical reason for doing so."

"What if I find you a new owner? Would you like that?"

"What? And give up my freedom?"

She laughed although she wasn't sure he meant to be funny. "As soon as we get back I'm going to call my great-grandmother and introduce myself and tell her all about you—if that's okay with you? She has a nice face; I think she'll say yes."

"What if she says *no*?" said Thaddeus.

High on the idea of saving Orvis, she had a sudden inspiration. "She can't. I won't give her the chance. I'll just say I'd like to see her before I go away. And that's the truth. If she says yes I'll go next weekend and take Orvis with me as a present. When she has a chance to get to know him, she'll want to keep him. If I can't find a home for myself, at least I can for him."

Thaddeus opened his mouth as if he were going to object, then didn't, but just stared at her. She could tell he wasn't too impressed by her idea. "What's wrong?"

"How are you going to get him there? Without being seen?"

"I'll find a way—if he wants to go."

"Do you want to go, Orvis?" Thaddeus asked.

"Your great-grandmother lives on Fisher's Isle? This is the possible destination you previously mentioned to me?" Orvis asked Toby.

"Yes," she said, grinning; she'd forgotten telling him that. "What do you think?"

"What is a great-grandmother?"

"The mother of my grandmother—my grandmother's name is Lillian."

"You are only a fourth-generation model?"

"Uh—no . . . I'll explain later. Do you want to go?"

Lights lit up over most of his body in erratic sequences and flashed on and off and on again. "Yes," he concluded.

Thaddeus ruffled his hair with both hands, obviously disturbed by the entire situation. "I don't think this is going to work," he said, "but can I come with you two? I can pay my own way; I've all sorts of credit. And maybe I can help you?"

"I'd like that," she said. "I'd like that very much."

SEVEN

The security system answered voice-only; her screen remained blank. "Fisher's Isle. Hugo III responding."

"Mrs. Philips, please. This is her great-granddaughter, Tabitha West."

"Place your fingertips on the console identiplate for security clearance, please."

Frowning, Toby obeyed. A snippet of music was interrupted by the computer's mellow voice. "Your prints are not included in our house index. Hold for a check of Federation Identity Archives." The music resumed. Minutes passed. "Identity confirmed and now in our file. I will see if Mrs. Philips wishes to speak with you. Please wait. Thank you."

She waited, hands cold with nerves. Maybe the old lady was taking a nap? Maybe she was sick? Or maybe she just didn't feel like speaking to any granddaughter of Lillian's.

If Lillian talked *to* her mother the same way she talked *about* her . . . Minutes passed.

Toby's screen suddenly lit up and there was the round, tanned face she vaguely remembered from the hologram. The woman looked anything but frail and her expression was one of amused curiosity. She seemed no more bothered by her unfashionable white hair and ample weight than she was by the fact that squinting in the sunlight made creases form around her eyes, or that her cheeks sagged at the jawline—all faults that Lillian said could be corrected in thirty minutes by any skilled youth clinician. Behind Mrs. Philips light glared off an expanse of water that stretched out to and blended with a blue-gray horizon. To the left of the screen pink geraniums spilled out of a hanging clay pot.

"It's rude, but I've been watching you for the past five minutes." The woman's voice was much younger than her appearance. "My excuse is that I wanted to see what your real face looked like, not the face you might wear for a stranger."

Toby wasn't sure she liked being spied on. "Do you approve?"

"It's a good face. You don't look like anyone in the family." Toby's giggle nearly drowned out the next remark. "We haven't met because I promised Lillian I wouldn't contact you. She thinks I'm a bad influence. 'Disturbing' was the word she used. You can call me Goldie; everyone in the family does. *Grandmother* or *great-grandmother* is such a mouthful as a title, don't you think? What are you called?"

"Toby. I don't like it, but it beats Tabitha."

"Not by much," Goldie said, laughing. "Now, suppose you tell me why you called me after you've been on the surface all this time?"

"I'd like to come and see you next weekend." Toby went on to explain about spring break and changing schools. Goldie listened without interrupting and when Toby ran out of words the old woman said nothing.

"Forgive me," she finally said, "if I tend to suspect there is more behind this call than what you've told me. But be that as it may, I'm delighted to hear from you and even more delighted that you want to visit. I'll send a car for you. And since this is a first meeting, you may want the moral support of the familiar—you're welcome to bring along a friend if you wish."

"Yes, please," said Toby. "I'd like that very much, thank you. His name is Thaddeus Hall. There's just one problem; could you send an airtruck? Maybe borrow one? There's a present I want to bring you—a surprise. It won't fit into a car. But don't tell that part to my Guardian when you talk to her," she added hurriedly. "You'll have to get her permission for me to go see you."

The woman's blue eyes narrowed and her left eyebrow arched. "A present so large you need a truck? That is something to look forward to."

By the time the conversation ended Toby felt better than she had in days. Not only was Orvis's problem nearly solved, but she liked the old lady very much and was looking forward to the visit. She hoped Goldie would like her

as a person, not just as a relative one felt one had a duty
to be polite to.

She waited until Dr. Ebert called before telling Thaddeus. Dr. Ebert had sounded glad to hear they were going,
as if giving Toby permission to make the trip somehow
compensated for the unpleasantness involved in her im-
pending transfer.

"It was so easy," Toby told Thaddeus later. "All I had
to do was call—and she's going to send an airtruck."

"How are we going to get Orvis in the truck?"

"In a freight container. Friday night. He can hide near
the loading dock and I'll get him loaded and ready to go."
She made a mental note to show Orvis her map of the
campus so he'd know where to meet her when he left his
hiding place in the landfill.

On Friday night the last bus left at nine. The campus was
quiet; most of the students had gone to the Art Club production of *Retale Space*, being staged in the little theater
in the Learning Center. An hour after curfew found Toby
dressed in black and hurrying along the Oval hedgerow on
her way to meet Orvis.

She was surprised to find she was not the only student
breaking the curfew. The first time she heard voices in the
darkness she shrank back into the prickly bushes, afraid a
guard had seen her, only to be passed by two seniors arm-
in-arm and too preoccupied with each other to notice anything else. There was another pair in the gazebo by the lily
pond and soft voices murmured and giggled from various
shrubberies she hurried past. She quickly skirted these as-

signations, promising herself she wasn't going to be that silly when she was a senior.

Next to the freight dock at the far edge of the landing field was an old brick building used as a repair and storage shed. To its left lay a yard where freight containers, usable aircar parts, and other salvaged junk were kept. It was here that Orvis was to meet her.

Pink security lights were on in the hangar where the Academy's airbus, utility vans, and some of the staff's private cars were housed. The bay doors were always left open unless it snowed, and the light cast a pale radiance over the gray field and its white guidelines. A feral cat walked across the tarmac, a blackness casting a long feline shadow with a waving tail. There was no sign or sound of people.

After making sure the loading dock was deserted and no one was lurking inside, she found an empty bin large enough to hold the robot and pushed it out onto the platform. The bin's nubby wheels were worn and stuck at the slightest excuse. She was afraid to give it a hard shove for fear of making them squeal or rumble. By the time she moved the bin out to where she wanted it she was sweating from nerves and effort.

Leaning against the bin and resting while the night air fanned her face, she heard what could have been spring peepers or the squeaking of Orvis's bad leg. The night was so dark that she couldn't see much beyond the edge of the platform. All at once a *thing* loomed up beside her. She gave a yelp of fright before seeing it was the robot, braced against the edge of the dock, its forelegs folded in against its body. All its lights were off.

"Is this the container you wish me to enter?"

With his speaker on low volume the question struck Toby like a silly line out of an old horror movie. She nearly giggled as she told him it was.

"It smells of cantaloupe."

"I know. I'm sorry but what difference does that make?"

"My olfactory sensors are as highly developed as my hearing and my vision. How would you like to be stuck inside a melon crate for hours?"

"But you can't get nauseous. You don't have a stomach."

"But I will stink of melon when I emerge. My potential owner may be revolted. My appearance is already a serious detriment to my acceptance. Would you be offended by a melon-scented robot?"

"I'd probably laugh," she admitted in a whisper. "Now climb up here and get in before anyone comes."

"I will use the ramp to the left of the platform. En route I will search for a less offensive container."

She gave a little sigh of exasperation as the robot backed away, dropped down onto all six of his legs, and faded into the shadows. It seemed to take a long time until she felt the weight of his footsteps on the platform.

"There is no other appropriately sized container."

"I know."

"You will explain the offensive odor to the potential owner?"

"Yes. I'll make her understand," she promised as she

released the catch and the end of the bin swung up for loading.

"I am unkempt again as well," Orvis complained.

"Don't worry," she said, "The truck will be here at eight in the morning and by noon tomorrow we'll be there. I'll make sure you have time to clean yourself before you meet Goldie."

"Thank you." Several tiny lights flashed. "The lemon oil was nice."

She took the hint. "I'll find some. Now please get in. The security guard will make the rounds soon."

Orvis reluctantly obeyed, sighing as he folded and telescoped himself into the space. The bent leg scraped against the side of the bin as he adjusted for its curvature. "You may close the unit," came his inhuman whisper from the darkness.

She locked the bin by entering her personal code number and name, and the shipping address, on the manifest keyboard. Where the board questioned *Contents*, she put "Rock samples for geology project." The weight sensors on the wheels reported the bin's contents at just under a half ton dry weight.

When their flight was called the next morning she and Thaddeus had been up for hours and were waiting in the boarding area, their bags stacked by their chairs. They had spent the past hour staring across the field at the dock where the freight bin stood alone. Twice a man had walked out onto the platform and they had tensed, waiting to see if their secret had been discovered, expecting to hear a Voice of Authority over the loudspeaker, summoning them to Dr. Milhaus's office and Doom.

The lounge was filling with field-trip students leaving on the eight o'clock airbus, all in a boisterous mood, talking and laughing, teasing one another and any student smaller than themselves. The only adult present was a young male instructor who had had the bad luck to draw supervisory duty on a Saturday morning. By the time he announced, "Private craft incoming; passengers West and Hall prepare to board from Gate One," both were tired from nerves and lost sleep.

They scrambled to their feet, hurriedly lifted their bags onto the loading belt, and followed them to the gate. The airtruck was just setting down and looked like a miniature green bus. On its left flank was the white logo of a tree in bloom and below it the legend "Lakeview Farms."

"Take a look!" an older boy called. "Rich Mama Toad sent her truck to bring Baby Toad home."

"He could hop home with his little girlfriend," suggested another, and there were a few snickers at this attempt at wit.

"Ignore them," Toby muttered. "We'll be outside in a minute." The truck was lumbering up to the gate.

"I'm gonna punch the big one in the mouth," said Thaddeus. "I can't go through my whole life ignoring everything."

"This isn't life, just school," she said, getting a firm grip on his wrist and wondering why boys always felt the need to fight. "When school is over you'll never see them again so why make them feel important by fighting with them now?"

"Because they insulted us now!" Thaddeus pulled free and was going to make good on his promise when the harassed instructor caught him by the arm, deftly swung him around, and thrust a clipboard in front of him to sign out. "I'll take care of them," he said. Thaddeus made a face, suspecting that meant nothing would be done.

"Hall, West," the instructor said hurriedly. "You're due back here by curfew tomorrow night. Academy rules require me to remind you that you cannot return with pets or other non-authorized possessions or communicable diseases. Prints here, please."

And then they were outside and the pilot was at the door of the truck to greet them. A tall gray-haired man dressed in a uniform of the same green and white as the truck, he was polite but unsmiling. "My name is Sanders. I'm Mrs. Philips's chauffeur. She said you had freight you wished to bring along?"

Her great-grandmother had a chauffeur? Toby frowned. Maybe the man was pretending. The name on the truck said Lakeview Farms, no mention of Goldie's name.

As he spoke, Sanders was loading their bags into the space behind the rear seat. Toby noticed the veins and cords bulging on his hands and neck. Here was another person letting himself age. Was that a new fashion on Earth?

"The container on the loading dock." She pointed.

Sanders frowned at first glance, the recovered himself. "Right."

Just to sit in the truck's worn passenger seats suggested a whole different way of life to Toby. Each habitat she'd ever been in had its own distinctive odor. All the Academy's buildings had a smell peculiar to the school. So, too, this truck smelled of its own world. As she folded the safety retainer around her she sniffed: cattle feed, onions, hay, leather seats, worn metal, and plastic. A thin film of yellow dust coated most of the cabin interior. She ran a finger over an armrest and left a clean streak.

As they bumped across the runway to the freight dock Sanders glanced back at them and apologized. "This isn't much of a treat to ride in, but you did request a truck."

"Yes, sir. It's fine," she said and knew she'd been right when she saw how easily the truck's hydraulic hoist loaded Orvis's bin.

"Something smells like rotten melon," Thaddeus complained as they lifted off.

"It was the only bin I could find empty."

"No wonder. Who would want it?"

Sanders touched a button and air began to hiss through the cabin. "We'll arrive in about three hours, Miss. There's no lavatory on board, so if you need to stop, don't hesitate to say so. There are sandwiches and drinks in the drawer beneath your seats."

From the air the solar roofs of Hillandale sparkled like sequined panels, and the greenhouse halls were crystal tubes connecting the main buildings. Like a huge necklace with the Learning Center as the main gem, Toby thought. She could see the paths worn by years of students walking through the woods and out to the landfill. It was easy to understand how Orvis had been seen from the air with all the leaves down. Not only had he been moving, but he would have cast a shadow, a most unusual shadow.

The truck banked, the Academy was left behind, and all she could see below was the nubby pink and apple-green canopy of new leaves and a river she'd never known was so close by. She glanced over to point it out to Thaddeus and was surprised to see him slumped into the window corner of his seat, already fast asleep, worn out by excitement. From the looks of him, he was going to sleep a long time.

Sanders was no company. Five minutes after takeoff he put the truck on autoguide and settled down to study a lesson tape of robo-serv repair. She could hear the instructor's voice whispering from his headset, interrupted now and then by announcements from air-traffic-control computer satellites orbiting miles overhead. A sigh escaped her, then a yawn. She wished she had brought something along to read. Or even something to study. Leaning back, she let her eyes fall shut and listened to the wind hissing past the truck.

Someone shook her. The cabin was too cold and smelled highly of melon. And stale sweat. An iron-hard thumb and thick fingers dug into her shoulder. Her eyes flew open and as quickly closed against a painful glare of sunlight. That brief glimpse told her they were on the ground, the door was open, the pilot's seat was empty, and a strange

man in a filthy gray jumpsuit was standing on the boarding
step, leaning in over her.

"Are we there yet?" Thaddeus's voice was blurred by
sleep. "What time is it?"

The grip on her shoulder tightened and she was yanked
off the seat and out the door. She missed the steps and
tripped over her own foot to fall sprawling onto the ground.
Dried weed stalks poked her stomach and her right knee
hurt. Only by instinctively putting her arms up to shield
her eyes had she saved her face from injury. Before she
could move, Thaddeus was thrown out. He tripped over her
feet and fell so hard that his teeth clacked together as his
chin hit the ground.

Too shocked to be afraid, she rolled over and was about
to sit up when she caught sight of Sanders and froze. The
chauffeur lay on his back, his arms outflung. There was
blood on the side of his forehead and more ran back onto
his gray hair. Standing over him, holding a stungun, was
another man in dirty clothing and battered boots. Sanders
was not moving and the armed man, whose hands and face
were as dirty as his clothes, seemed pleased with himself.

Thaddeus grunted softly, took a deep sighing breath, and
stirred. Before the man with the gun could turn to see, she
gripped the boy's arm and pressed her face against his head.
"Pretend you're unconscious," she breathed into his ear.
"Keep your eyes shut. They might kill us, too."

Thaddeus went rigid.

EIGHT

He's got a bin of rocks back here," a man called. The truck springs creaked. "Weighs half a ton."

"How'd you know it's rocks?" said the man with the gun.

"Because *I* can read, stupid. His name's Toby West. Must be some kind of science person or something."

After a string of obscenities, some of which Toby had never heard before, the other man added, "And don't call me stupid. Maybe I can't read but I'm the one smart enough to get him down here and get us another truck. Dump the damn bin and let's go. He might have told someone he was coming down."

"What if the rocks are worth something?"

"What'd we do with 'em if they was? Dump 'em!"

"How about his kids?"

"How about 'em? They're a hunnert miles from no-where."

"They seen us."

"So what? Who they gonna tell out here?"

There was a rattle and a slam, followed by several loud thumps. Opening one eye a crack, Toby saw the freight bin slide out, fall to the ground, and tip over. The bay door slid shut and locked.

"You know how to fly this thing?" asked the armed man.

"No problem. They'll never make a machine I can't han-dle."

"This one's a lot heavier than ours. I'm taking the pilot."

"You don't trust me you can stay here."

"Whoa!" The gun swung toward the truck.

"Okay. Okay. So we can dump the old man later. Hey, lookie! Food!"

"Up, old man. You ain't hurt bad. Not as bad as you could be. On your feet! Let's move."

She heard the grass rustle and caught a glimpse of San-ders—stooped and staggering, but alive—being pushed to-ward the truck. That wasn't fair; they were half his age and had a gun.

"You stop that!" she yelled without thinking. "You just stop that! He's hurt and you're hurting him more!" She scrambled to her feet and ran at the armed man—who sim-ply waited until she got close enough before kicking side-ways with a boot that caught her on the left thigh. As she fell she saw Sanders stumble up the step and fall onto the rear seat of the cab. The man in the truck laughed and Toby felt an insane urge to destroy him in any way she could.

Thaddeus sprang to his feet and ran, launching himself into the air and driving his right foot into the back of the armed man's left knee. The man's leg collapsed but he caught hold of the doorframe and twisted and swung his gun arm back, striking the boy a glancing blow to the upper body that was hard enough to knock him down.

"Damn kids," said the man as he pulled himself inside. "Let's get out of here before I have to hurt 'em."

The cab door slid shut, the motor hummed to life, and the truck lifted off, blowing dust and old grass in their faces. They watched helplessly as it moved from sight over the nearby forest.

They were in the center of a field of poverty grass, surrounded by hardwood forest on three sides and scrub and weeds on the fourth. About fifty feet behind them stood an old, incredibly dirty red airtruck, its freight bay door missing, its windows cracked and muddy, and its frame sagging heavily to the left side. Except for a few crows and two turkey buzzards circling high overhead, there was no sign of life.

Toby sat up and looked at her shaking knees. Her clothes were muddy and grass-stained and she had a sour taste in her mouth. She had wanted to look so nice when she first met her great-grandmother. "It was so easy," she remembered telling Thaddeus. And now they were lost here. With no coats, and no food, and wearing dress boots. Tears burned into her eyes and she blinked them away. Crying wouldn't help. Besides, she was older than Thaddeus and he wasn't crying. She glanced at him to make sure and saw him looking the other way. Her knees hurt, and her thigh throbbed where she'd been kicked. When she shifted her weight to ease the pain, her heels jerked in the grass. As hard as she tried to make them stop, they wouldn't. She looked at Thaddeus again to see if he'd noticed and saw he was shaking as much as she.

"Are you hurt?" she said.

"Bruised. You?"

"Yes. And scared. Very scared." She decided she might as well be honest.

"Me, too." He looked toward the woods, his face pale. "We could die out here."

"Not right away." Somehow saying it aloud didn't make it sound as comforting as the idea was when she thought it.

"I don't understand." He was making an effort to act grown up about their situation. "How did this happen? How did we get here? Who were those people?"

"I don't know. I fell asleep, too." The sight of a large weed splinter protruding from the back of her left wrist distracted her and she fell silent to pull it out. The sliver left a gray streak under the skin that slowly filled with blackish blood. She sucked the wound and spit, then cleaned the scrape on her knee the same way. The phrase "a hundred miles from nowhere" kept running through her mind. "Those men must be truck thieves," she said aloud.

"Really?"

"You don't have to be sarcastic."

A sharp crack made them both jump. The freight bin had rolled and struck a rock. One side had split open.

"Orvis!" She'd almost forgotten about him. She started to jump up at her customary speed but pain forced a cry of "Ahhh!" and a more careful rising. By the time she was on her feet the hexagonal bin had tipped again and the lid end had fallen off. Two metal legs reached out; toes dug claw-like into the ground and anchored. With much scraping, the robot pulled himself free of the battered remains of the container and lay on the ground like an insect resting after escape from a chrysalis.

"Are you all right?"

"I am undamaged. I will, however, require four minutes to clear my olfactory sensors of the odor of melon. After that I shall rise. Keep back, please."

After what had just happened to them, the idea that he could still fuss about the smell of melons struck her as funny. She began to giggle and couldn't stop and soon wasn't sure if she was laughing or crying.

"Do you know how we got here, Orvis? Could you hear anything?" asked Thaddeus, careful not to look at her.

"Yes."

At that Toby took a deep breath and managed to control herself. Making sure Thaddeus didn't see, she wiped tears away with the back of her hand. When the robot didn't continue Thaddeus said, "Come on! Why did Sanders land out here?"

"Ignorance. Any novice spacer would know better than to solo respond to an automatic SOS. Research shows 43.2

percent of such calls are pirate bait. Our pilot also neglected to notify E-band of his unscheduled landing, and, if I am not mistaken, he was initially off course at his time of response to the SOS. Result: he made his craft available for hijacking. Sanders doesn't get out much—as my sixth owner would say."

"How would a robot know—"

"This robot was once a frequent flyer, having had two owners who were experienced pilots. When it comes to flying, Sanders is strictly local."

Toby interrupted. "He got an SOS from that old truck?"

Orvis raised himself on his front legs for a better view before answering. "Yes. The condition of the vehicle explains the weakness of the transmitter."

"It's still transmitting?"

"Yes. Weakly."

It was the first good news she'd heard since she got here and she set off at a limping run across the field. The grass was trampled flat around the truck and strewn with litter. Inside the truck was no neater. The partition between the passenger and freight area was gone, the cabin was filthy, the seats broken and torn. The communications system had been ripped out of the control board and the hole was stuffed with trash. She stepped in and leaned over the pilot's seat and her nose wrinkled in disgust at the smell of stale tar-beer and sweat exuding from the upholstery. Behind the dust and fingerprints coating the control board one red button slowly blinked: the automatic emergency beeper. Orvis had been right!

"So all we have to do now is wait to get rescued." Thaddeus climbed into the open freight bay, his footsteps making musical *boinks* on the worn floor. "How long do you think those two men waited?" He kicked a plastic beer can out into the grass.

"Four days," said Orvis, who had followed.

"How do you know that?"

With maddening deliberateness, designating them Speakers A, B, and The Pilot, the robot recited the dialogue he'd overheard while trapped inside his bin. He even included the obscenities, which both children found extremely interesting. What it all amounted to was that Sanders had offered the two men a ride to the nearest town, where they might catch an airbus or find a wrecker to come and get their truck. One of the men had pretended to faint from hunger and Sanders, attempting to aid him, was struck on the head. "We never pay to fly, old man. Waiting here four days earned us this truck," Speaker A had said after hitting Sanders.

"Sanders said 'the nearest town,' " said Toby. "What is that?"

Orvis's lights blinked. "We are forty miles off course and approximately one hundred miles southwest of that point. I can locate Fisher's Isle. However, my data base contains only a topographic area map which may be obsolete."

"But what is the nearest town?"

"I do not know," said Orvis.

"If where we're going is only a hundred miles, we could walk it," said Thaddeus.

Toby stared at him. He was not joking. Her concept of distance was based on her life in the habitats; the largest she'd ever seen was fifty miles long with pods four miles wide. That had seemed so enormous to her that to even think of walking twice that far was absurd. "Do you know how *far* that is?"

"Sure. One hundred times the length of the ship where I was born. Some of the crew ran the track around the inside of the hull ten times every day. It didn't take them that long. And five times how long it took them—"

"But that was flat and enclosed and they had food and water."

"I didn't say we *had* to do it. Just that we probably could if we had to." Thaddeus looked down and scratched a mosquito bite. She saw him biting his lip and wondered if he was so scared he wanted to cry, or if thinking of his ship made him sad in addition to being scared.

"We got tired coming back from the landfill," she said more gently.

"Because we're still not used to Earth-grav. Besides, you can be tired and still walk if you have to."

"The SOS transmitter has ceased to function," announced Orvis.

Toby suddenly felt very, very tired and her stomach hurt. She sat down on the floor of the freight bay and stared out at the littered grass. For several minutes none of them said a word, till desperation overcame despair.

"Orvis? Can you signal a satellite for rescue? Don't you contain emergency equipment?"

"Yes. But not for use on Earth."

"Why not?"

"No satellite orbiting this planet is programmed to acknowledge my emergency signal. It would be mere noise to them."

"If they sent you to Jupiter's moons and asteroids and places like that, didn't they put a location finder into you?"

"I can respond to a signal. I cannot initiate contact."

She frowned, confused. "How did they pick you up?"

"They could not pick me up. When my mission was completed, I returned to the bay of the lander unit and reattached myself. The lander's boosters lifted me out to the orbit of the research ship for intercept. I did not require an emergency beacon. Robots do not have emergencies. No." He paused and his turret moved. "A red-tailed hawk is hunting at the edge of the forest. I must study it at closer range."

She still frowned as she watched him walk away. It was that final, unnecessary "No" that struck her as odd. And part of what he said didn't make sense. Had he been human she would have been sure he was lying. If he did contain an emergency signal and used it, and they were rescued by strangers, he would betray his continued existence and might get sent back to the dump, or worse. And he knew that. Almost against her will she remembered all the things Dr. Milhaus had said, and how worried he had looked.

But could robots lie? When a lie endangered human life?

Lie to protect themselves? Or could Orvis, since he was a discriminating robot? He seemed so honest.

"Do you think he'll come back?" Thaddeus sounded worried. "I mean, he's safer out here than almost anyplace. He can go anywhere now, just like he was going to in the first place."

Thaddeus confirmed her fears. The fact that they wouldn't be in this predicament if they hadn't tried to help him meant nothing to a robot, Toby thought. You couldn't expect a robot to care. "He'll come back." She spoke with more optimism than she felt. "He wouldn't leave us alone out here."

"Why not?" said Thaddeus. "Everyone else does. Why should a robot be any different? I don't know about you, but there's not one person on Earth who would really care if I was lost or not. My Guardian at school would care only because losing a kid would look bad on his record. The bank wouldn't care. My parents might, but they're so far away that I'd be eighty-five years old before they got the message and a hundred and seventy before they got back."

She'd never really understood the time involved in deep-space travel, traveling at light-speed for light-years. She couldn't be sure if Thaddeus would be that old or not, but thinking about him kept her from wondering about her own parents' reaction. She suspected their first response would be anger, not worry—especially when they heard where she'd been headed when the accident occurred. And having something happen to her while they were on location would be so inconvenient; she could almost hear them complaining: "Couldn't she get herself lost during hiatus, when we'd have time to worry about it?"

But there was no point in saying this to Thaddeus. Talking to outsiders about family faults might gain temporary sympathy, but sooner or later people remembered that *you* were part of that family you complained about. And if your family was so terrible, you might not be so wonderful yourself.

Thaddeus was looking at her, waiting for an answer, for reassurance. Because he expected her to reassure him, even though she was just as frightened as he was, she tried to do so. "I would care if you were lost," she said. "I care what happens to you. And you care about me, or you wouldn't have asked to come along. And we both care what happens to Orvis, so none of us is alone. I know that isn't much help, but it's the best I can do without just lying to make you feel better."

When he turned away she thought he didn't believe her anyway and she was sorry she'd said she cared. But then he turned back again and she saw tears in his eyes. He reached out awkwardly for her right hand and touched it tentatively, then gripped and shook it as if sealing a bargain. His hand felt small and warm and dry. "Thank you." He brushed at his eyes with his free hand and looked embarrassed.

"Why are you thanking me?"

"For liking me. For admitting you do." He paused, then whispered, "Most people here don't."

"I think they do—or would—if they had a chance to

know you. You're a nice person. But anyway, you're welcome." To end the awkwardness she took refuge in their situation. "So what do you think we should do?"

He shrugged, let go of her hand, and sat down beside her on the freight bay floor. "When we don't arrive your great-grandmother will probably call the Academy and then the Air Patrol."

"And then Dr. Ebert will have to call my parents. And Lillian will get into an uproar—"

"What happens when she gets into an uproar?"

"She makes everybody more upset than she is . . ." Toby paused with newly gained appreciation of her grandmother's character.

"And things get done *fast*."

"You think we should wait here?"

"For a while," she said. "They're sure to search for us. Besides, what choice do we have?"

When the two children fell silent Orvis listened to the faint cries of the hawk circling high above the field. The voices of hunting raptors seemed to him to be out of character with the rest of their personalities; the weak mewing cries conflicted with cruel talons and curved beaks. So, too, much of what the children said and did conflicted with human behavior as he understood it. Unlike the physically mature humans he had known, these two repeatedly used the words *care* and *feel*. Each time they did so, he had to refer to his dictionaries and thesaurus. Both words were extremely imprecise. Based on observable data, when the children said *feel* in reference to himself, they meant *to have sympathy or pity for*. Both *sympathy* and *pity* had imprecise meanings. The word *care*, as they used it, most logically referred to *interest in or concern for* a unit's proper and continued functioning, with a shared meaning element of *liking*, or *preference for one's companionship*, or *responsibility for*.

Orvis mulled this over. If they *cared* about him, did they also *feel* him? Sympathy and pity were *feelings*. Unclear. The sensory fibers on his legs allowed him to *feel* obstructions in his path. Was the children's understanding of the word *feel* an extension of similar sensory capacities? Did adult humans possess such capacities? They junked what was of no further use. Yet these children said they *cared* what happened to him. Why did they assume a robot would *care* about them? And if they did not *care*, would they attempt to find him a safe haven?

Safe haven? Distracted by the term, Orvis searched briefly to see why it was in his vocabulary and discovered several spy novels he had neglected to erase after scanning the texts years earlier.

Humans were as confusing in reality as they were in the books of fiction the rare-book dealer had advised him to read. The man had said he was too logical, that emotional content was completely wasted on him. In an effort to make sense of illogical human actions in the stories, Orvis had scanned dozens of books on human psychology. These left him equally flummoxed but he had retained the data for future reference. He did a rapid review of these books. If humans could build minds as logical as his own, how could they allow such chaos in their own living minds? He found no answer.

Summary and conclusion: the children's response to him was not logical, according to data available. Still, his only field observations were of adults. Perhaps immature humans were different? Orvis sighed. Walking on Io had been easier than this. Before his life with humans all he had to worry about was picking up geological samples while avoiding being frozen or trapped in ice chasms. But here a robot could short-out while attempting to assimilate and make sense of the fragments of knowledge necessary to understand humans temporarily.

Orvis sent his musings to Storage. They served no purpose now, but sometimes thoughts put into Storage reassembled and assumed their own sequential logic and, if recalled, made unexpected sense. Much like some human dreams, if F. W. Boyd's book *The Function of Dreams* was still valid.

Wind whistled through stiff feathers. Orvis focused on the hawk plummeting in perfect grace; listening sensors recorded a stiff *thunk*, a rabbit's death cry, and camera eyes watched the hawk lumber back into the air, grace gone, carrying its twitching prey to devour on an elm snag.

Noon came and went, and afternoon, and evening. No one came. No aircraft passed overhead in any direction. Orvis did not return.

To pass the time and to keep from thinking, they explored the clearing and decided a large building and landing field once stood there. Beneath the weeds and grass was clay studded with pavement rubble. Cement patches of an old highway scarred the scrub growth from east to west. There were blackberry thickets just coming into leaf and wild blueberry bushes. Both were months from bearing fruit. When they stopped to drink from a pond in a marshy spot, frogs plopped into the muddy-tasting water. Then, for want of anything else to do, they went back to the wrecked airtruck and sat down again to wait. Toby fell asleep in the sun and Thaddeus soon joined her. Cold and their empty stomachs woke them at sunset.

The April afternoon had been almost warm but with sunset the temperature dropped. Fog formed in the low spots. A sliver of new moon was setting when silent deer came out of the woods to graze. Suddenly the shaggy-antlered buck snorted, ears flicked to attention, and the herd fled, their white tails bobbing as they ran.

Standing up to see what had caused the panic, the children saw Orvis coming toward them. Both breathed a deep sigh of relief. The robot was walking oddly. As he came closer in the dusk they saw that, tucked beneath his body and secured by his mid-legs, he was half-carrying and half-dragging a load of dead branches, some of them quite large. Without a word he stopped beside the truck and let the wood fall onto the grass.

"What is that for?" asked Thaddeus.

"It is for building a fire. It was one of my duties when I was Going Camping with my previous owner."

To their immense interest, using a forefoot as a rake, the robot scraped bare a patch of ground and in the center of the bald spot placed two of the largest logs, then rested three smaller pieces atop them, like a crude bench. Beneath the bench he raked smaller twigs and pieces of litter. Revealing a laser in his turret, he aimed a beam at the kindling. The paper smoked and began to curl. Flames suddenly licked up.

"Fire provides warmth, light, and serves as a beacon for aircraft," said Orvis.

"Wow!" said Thaddeus, impressed. As he began to warm himself by the flames he suddenly recalled Orvis's first camping story.

"Are there bears around here?"

"I do not know."

"Did you see any big animals out there in the woods?"

"Yes."

"Any dangerous animals?" There were times when Orvis's cryptic answers irritated Toby. But then, so did hunger.

"I saw a cat," said Orvis.

"Cats aren't dangerous."

Orvis put a foot into the fire to adjust one of the top logs. "In her definitive study on the carnivores surviving or replenishing themselves on the North American continent, A. K. Bundy, Ph.D., writes that this species of cat, depending on the locale, is called puma, cougar, panther, mountain lion, or the archaic *catamount*. Color: gray, brown, pale yellow. Weight: from one hundred thirty to two hundred fifty pounds. Range: North and South American continents. The estimated weight of the specimen just sighted is one hundred fifty pounds. I do not know the name used in this locale," concluded Orvis.

"You *really* saw a cat that big?" Thaddeus was wide-eyed.

"Aren't they extinct?" Toby was on tiptoe, nervously scanning the tree line, suddenly aware that the bushes provided concealing ground cover until very close to the truck. She nearly cried out in fright when Thaddeus jumped down from the truck and grabbed one of the branches to use as a club. "Do you see it?" she asked.

"No. Is it coming?" He jumped back onto the freight bed.

"No," said Orvis. "It was feeding on a dead deer and attempting to communicate with the body with rasping vocalizations. It fled at my approach."

Neither slept much that night. The ridged metal floor of the freight bay grew icy cold and they had to move back into the cab. The foul-smelling seats at least kept them warmer than the floor. The seats could be swiveled, allowing them to rest their feet on the bench seat, which they did.

When Thaddeus dozed off Toby felt completely alone and vulnerable. In a basic way she couldn't have expressed she understood now most ex-Terrans' fear of Earth, and especially The Empty. Out here you couldn't ignore the fact that Earth was so large, so indifferent. If she was here, or on Mars—or dead—the sun would still come up, summer would come again, and fall. And Earth would be here long after every human and every habitat were gone and forgotten.

There was a special quality to the quiet that puzzled her until she realized that for the first time in her life, she couldn't hear a single machine. Aside from her own and Thaddeus's breathing there was no human sound. But there were sounds, and each time her eyes closed in exhaustion, one of those sounds would waken her.

Things were walking around out there, in the woods, in the grass. Branches cracked, feet scuffled through leaves. Paws padded over clay and animals stopped to sniff and perhaps watch. She tried to remember what animals the zoos had released back to the wild but thinking about that made her even more uneasy. In the distance deer were barking, although she didn't recognize the sound and was frightened of it, too. The howling of wild dogs couldn't be mistaken. Twice Thaddeus moaned and tried to talk in his sleep, his words incoherent but desperate. When she patted his arm he fell silent again. She longed for her own bed, her safe room.

When the fire died down and the stars were so bright that they could be seen through the dirty windows, something screamed in the woods. It was a sound so terrible that she stopped breathing while it lasted. Starting on a shriek and descending down into a caterwaul of sobbing, it ended in a series of raspy coughs—like a woman gone mad and choking on grief and murder. When the cry ended it left the night completely still.

After what seemed like an hour but was less than seconds she heard Orvis's turret click softly and she dared to breathe again. "Was that human?" she whispered. She could hear her racing heartbeat in her ears.

"No."

"What was it then?"

"Possibly a large cat."

Thaddeus's chair creaked as he reached over and gripped her hand tightly. Then, wordlessly, he got up and she slid over to make room for him. Both felt better in one chair, and warmer. But not much. In time he dozed off again and his head slumped against her shoulder. His hair smelled of the Academy's shampoo and of the pines he'd brushed against that afternoon. She hesitated, then rested her cheek against his soft curls. He sighed and snuggled closer.

She took comfort from his trust and from the fact that Orvis stood beside the freight bay, his shadow on the inner wall growing fainter as the fire burned down and darker when he added new branches to the ashy coals.

"Someone will come in the morning." She kept repeating the line to herself silently, over and over. "Someone will come in the morning."

Was the robot truly keeping watch over them, she wondered, or did he just prefer that location for the night? Maybe his former owner trained him to tend campfires? No. It was better to believe that he stood there because he cared, because he knew that nothing bad could get past him and hurt them if he stood there. If he cared. If the cat was real. If . . .

The last sound she heard before sleep finally came was the squeak of his bad leg as he bent to add another log to the fire.

NINE

She woke and moaned softly, realizing where she was. She was hungry, stiff, and sore, and itching from mosquito bites. The sun was up. Birds sang with blithe disregard for her misery.

"You forget things when you sleep." Thaddeus was sitting on the bench seat watching her, patiently waiting for her to waken and keep him company. "The first couple months after I came to Earth I hated to wake up. In my dreams I was still home, on the ship, and everything was— like it should be. Sometimes I . . ." He gave a self-deprecating shrug and smiled, as if to deny how much he still wanted his past life.

"If I ever have a child I'm going to keep it with me until it wants to go," vowed Toby. "No matter how old it gets or where I go."

"Me, too." He scratched a mosquito bite on his left

cheek, sniffed the ribbed cuff of his jacket, and announced, "I stink! Let's go outside and air ourselves."

"Where's Orvis?" She picked up two empty beer cans to use for water. As an afterthought Thaddeus picked up his club.

"Off in the woods somewhere. His screeching leg's what woke me."

"He stayed in front of the door all night."

"I saw."

Thoughts of the big cat and the memory of that scream in the night made them newly cautious. Embarrassed but desperate, they took turns standing guard with the club while the other went behind the bushes. In an attempt at basic cleanliness they washed in one cold little pond and drank from the next. Toby's teeth felt furry and she broke a green twig off a wild cherry tree and used the splintered end as a toothbrush. The raw wood's bitter flavor was a definite improvement over the taste in her mouth.

"I'm so hungry I could eat raw oysters." It was the most disgusting thing Thaddeus could imagine.

"There's frogs," said Toby. "People eat frogs' legs in the colonies. They're very expensive—like cultured dandelion greens for salads."

Thaddeus made a face. "We'd have to catch them—and kill them—and cook them . . ." When she nodded at each step, he asked, "Could you?"

"I dissected frogs in biology. I guess I could. Can you?"

"Maybe we'll hear an aircar soon and I won't have to find out."

Both scanned the morning sky. Small puffy clouds drifted from horizon to horizon. Six crows and a blue jay chased a hawk that seemed indifferent to the harassment. A pair of starlings passed over. But they saw no aircraft.

"Do you get the feeling that wherever they're hunting for us, it's not in the right place?" she said, hating to admit her fear.

"It's still early in the morning."

"They should have found us yesterday."

"Mr. Sanders didn't escape. Or they killed him."

"Or he didn't know where he left us."

Thaddeus ruffled his hand through his hair to conceal his distress. "Okay," he said, but with no great enthusiasm, "let's catch some frogs. If we have to walk out, we'll need the energy, and if we wait too long to eat we'll get weak. I'm a little dizzy now."

"Me, too," Toby admitted. She didn't tell him her stomach hurt because she wasn't sure if the cause was physical. Besides, what could he do about it except worry?

He proved to be far the better frog-catcher, his methods inelegant but effective. She was unwilling to risk her body in the pursuit, but he would see a frog and throw himself on it so quickly that even when the frog jumped, four times out of seven he fell on it.

Two of his victims died on impact. She dispatched the other unfortunates with a rock, a rather messy business that made her gag. After that trauma she was fairly cool about finding a table rock and a glass shard to use as a knife. Noting that when stretched out on their backs there was a distressingly human look to frogs, she apologized to each one for what she had to do. The glass shard was not the best of knives. By the time she'd removed and skinned the legs and lined them up on a bark platter, she'd lost any appetite she had.

For want of utensils they skewered the legs on green sticks, poked the sticks into the ground, and bent them over the fire. Juice dripped into the flames and smoked. The smell of the meat as it cooked was not tempting.

"What did those dirty men eat?" Thaddeus wondered aloud. "They didn't make a fire."

"Beer." She kicked a can out of her way.

"That's all?"

"From the looks of things. Besides, remember how glad he was to find our sandwiches and drinks?"

The memory of sandwiches was almost more than Thaddeus could bear. "I hope they crash!" he said bitterly.

"Sanders is with them."

"Then I hope they get caught and sent to the worst place there is."

Not sure when the meat was done, they overcooked it. One leg fell into the coals and had to be raked out. That was the best one Toby ate. At least the ashes gave some flavor to the dried-out chickenlike meat. Each time she caught a whiff of the smell of raw frog on her hands she wanted to gag. It was not her idea of breakfast.

Although the food did make them feel better, by mid-morning the idea of having to catch and eat more frogs prompted them to start walking. Orvis returned while they were kicking dirt over the fire.

"The fire serves as a beacon," he said as smoke roiled up. "Why are you extinguishing the flames?"

"We're leaving," Tody said. "The fire might escape and spread."

"That would create a larger beacon," said Orvis.

"Nobody is looking for us. If they were, they would have been here by now. Do you see any aircraft?"

"No," said Orvis.

"So we're going to walk out."

She used the glass shard to scratch a message on the side of the old truck just in case rescuers found it:

4/5/43—We are walking west on old highway. Going to Fisher's Isle.

> Tabitha West
> Thaddeus Hall
> (The Hillandale Academy, NE 10)

"You think anyone will ever read that?" Thaddeus said as he watched her pocket the shard after wrapping it in a piece of discarded sheet plastic.

"I hope so." She picked up the beer can she'd used to gather water and stuffed it under her jacket waistband in lieu of a pocket large enough to hold it. He hesitated, then followed her example. He also took his club.

Both walked away from the scrapped truck looking far more confident than they felt. Bad as that truck was, it was still a form of shelter as well as the only other link with humankind in this wilderness.

Orvis led the way. Walking faster than she'd ever seen him go, he was soon far ahead. "Orvis! Wait up!" she called, but he would not stop.

"Maybe he doesn't want to be with us? Maybe we smell too bad?" said Thaddeus. "I mean, the melons really bothered him."

"I think I insulted him," she said. "In his logic he may think I didn't appreciate the fire. I shouldn't have been so grumpy. If he isn't bothered by the heat on Venus, why would he even think about a grass fire? We wouldn't if we hadn't been taught to. And if we didn't burn."

"That's true, huh?" Thaddeus jumped from one patch of concrete to the next. "What you're afraid of depends on what you are. Do you think Orvis is afraid of anything?"

"What would scare you if you were Orvis?"

"Not much. Getting torn apart, or blown up . . ." Thaddeus linked his thumbs behind his back as he walked. "It would be fun to be that strong," he decided. "Nobody would pick on you. Or call you stupid names. Why did they call these wide roads highways? It's no higher than anything around and it runs between some of the hills."

"I don't know." She was confused by the abrupt change of subject. "You can look it up when we get back to school."

"You think we'll ever get back?"

"Sure. These roads all led somewhere once. Some of the towns are still there if we walk far enough."

"But how far is that?"

Just past Thaddeus's head she caught a glimpse of what could have been a big yellow dog slinking through the bushes. Did dogs have hair that short and shiny? She ran a few steps, hoping for another look, and then saw that Orvis had finally stopped. His turret glinted as it rotated and then he stepped left and began to circle back toward them, still moving faster than usual. "Danger!" His volume was so loud she jumped with fright. "Keep walking." The words echoed back from the forest.

"What's wrong? said Thaddeus. "Why is he so loud?"

"I don't know. It may be the big cat."

"Where?" He craned his neck to see over the bushes around them. "I can't see anything."

As he spoke, a yellow-brown cougar emerged into plain view no more than twenty feet ahead, raised itself to its full height, and lashed its long tail. It was looking at the robot, curious. In spite of Orvis's warning, both of them stopped and stared open-mouthed with awe.

Toby had never seen so beautiful a creature. Zoos dulled them somehow, she thought, but this one gleamed in the sunlight and its flanks rippled with muscles with each move it made.

"Danger!" boomed Orvis.

The cat was still watching the robot approach and did not like what it saw. At the loud "Danger!" its ears went flat and the tip of its tail began to twitch nervously. A guttural questioning *UR-R-rrh* was followed by a deeper chest growl. As Orvis came closer the cat flexed its paws against the ground, started to feint into a crouch, and then thought better of that.

With a squawl of angry dismay it wheeled and ran straight toward them.

Whether the animal had forgotten their presence, being frightened by the robot, or whether it wished to intimidate was unclear. What was plain was that—with no apparent effort—it leaped over them.

Instinctively ducking, Toby got a wide-eyed view of stiff beige whiskers on a pink and white muzzle, eyes like clear yellow gems, huge clawed paws, and a pale furry belly. Landing with a soft thud, the cougar kicked a spray of gravel bits as it bounded away into the brush.

"It's a female," she whispered when the cat seemed safely beyond hearing. "It's nursing kittens."

"You *looked?*" said Thaddeus, awestruck by this degree of self-possession.

"It went right over us. You couldn't help but notice."

"Not me. I shut my eyes. If I'm going to get killed, I don't want to see it coming. Especially not with teeth."

They were so intent on watching the bushes where the cat had disappeared that neither paid attention to Orvis until he stopped beside them. "In her definitive work on the carnivores of North America, A. K. Bundy described these cats as highly defensive of their territory," he said.

Toby mentally translated. "You mean, it may come back?"

"Yes."

"But it's afraid of you."

"You are edible."

"Oh." If she thought about that now she would faint. "Would you walk near us, please?"

"Yes."

"We shouldn't be out here." Thaddeus was mussing his hair in agitation, his face pale. "We don't belong here! Maybe people did once, but not now! I never wanted to come to Earth! I never wanted to stay! I never wanted—"

"We're okay," Toby said. "We're okay. We're not hurt." She caught hold of his hand and gave him a playful tug even though she didn't feel playful at all. "Don't get all upset. Let's just keep moving and we can make our plans as we go along."

Thaddeus looked at her as if he weren't going to buy this unwarranted reassurance. But after initially hanging back, he allowed himself to be pulled along. "Orvis," she went on, "you used a laser to start the fire last night. Do you have any other weapons?"

"The laser is not a weapon. It is an Analytic Systems Tool used in conjunction with the spectrographic—"

"Do you have other *tools* that could help us?"

"My basic equipment includes two lasers, one for chemical analysis of rock samples, one for cutting samples or melting impediments; a stungun to aid in retrieval of live alien specimens of less than two hundred pounds in weight; power tools consisting of socket wrenches, screwdrivers, a punch, drill bits, and a small pneumatic hammer. The power tools are not original equipment. They were added by my first private owner, an aged physicist who wanted some help with her hobbies. She said I wasn't friendly enough to suit her. She sold me to the rare-book dealer and bought herself a cocker spaniel."

"Can you kill animals?" asked Thaddeus, without so much as a smile.

Orvis sighed. "The hi-stun is linked to my vision. When a life form comes into viewing range, the creature's approximate speed and mass are computed and the force necessary to render the life form immobile is automatically calculated. I do not kill. I stun."

"But could you kill?" she persisted. "Could you kill that cat if you had to keep it from killing us?"

Orvis had to think this over for some time. "Yes. I am free now. The cutting laser and the hi-stun would kill if safety levels were exceeded."

Thaddeus breathed a sigh of relief. "Would you kill to help us?"

"Kill what to help you?"

"Small animals? For food? So we could eat. If we can't find frogs we'll starve."

"You want me to kill frogs?"

"No. Birds and rabbits. We can kill the frogs."

Orvis absorbed this with side lights blinking. "Do you require food now?"

"By evening."

"Noted."

"If you can carry two hundred pounds, could you give Toby and me a ride?" Thaddeus was seeing the robot from a more practical point of view. "We don't weigh two hundred pounds together."

"Your combined weight is approximately one hundred seventy-two pounds," said Orvis. "Assume a prone position. Offer no resistance. I will secure you in place after lifting."

Toby's eyes met Thaddeus's; both thought the same thing: "You're going to carry us like you carried the firewood?" she said.

"Yes. Your appendages may drag."

"Why can't we ride on your back?"

Orvis's lights blinked rapidly. "I was not designed to be a common carrier. I am not a mode of transportation."

At ground level their view was limited to woodland. Within a period of five centuries the land they walked had gone from forest to farm to industry and, when the Industrial Age ended, to high-density-population urban towers. Colonial expansion had emptied the towers; man and time had razed them. Now the scar of the highway was the only sign of humankind's once total occupation of this landscape, and soon that would be erased. As the years passed and the tall trees returned, the groundwater level rose again and creeks had reasserted themselves by cutting across the roadbed, creating deep gullies. Frost and tree roots slowly crumbled the road's surface. Twice they saw shaggy wild red cattle drinking from water holes, and once brown-and-white goats watched them from a hillside.

They had stopped to rest beside a stream in late afternoon when Orvis heard what he said were pheasants. Leaving them to wait for him beneath a tree, he went off to hunt.

"If he shoots anything, do I have to get it ready to eat?" asked Thaddeus. "I mean, you did the frogs. It's my turn." She nodded and he made a face. "Okay. I just wanted to make sure. I'll do it, but I don't want to. Seeing where food comes from makes me sick. Especially meat. On a ship you just press buttons and dinner comes out all ready to eat. I liked that much better."

"Me, too. I'm sorry I got us into this."

"Don't take credit for what you didn't do. Besides, I asked to come along. And when we get to where we're going, we'll have something to talk about. I'll bet we're the only people we know who ever killed and ate frogs, for example."

"And I'll bet nobody will envy us," she said and they both laughed.

When rested, they gathered firewood and tried to stack it as Orvis had the night before. The only difference was Orvis could carry logs; what they collected was large kindling. Toby recalled a script where campers had made a spit with forked branches and a long cross branch. She managed to build a crude imitation. Things were harder without studio technicians in the wild, she noted, but at least that film scene was real enough to teach her something they could use to survive. By the time Orvis returned, both were feeling more confident.

Two pheasants dangled from Orvis's mid-feet. When he lay the birds on the firewood, the ashy spots left by the laser on their feathers scarcely showed.

"I have gained new understanding," he announced. "I have learned why some humans refuse to kill. My rare-book dealer and stockbroker owners both tried to explain this to me, why some humans hunt or take part in wars. And why some do not. I did not understand until I had caused death. Specifically, I caused the death of birds. My action turned grace and flight into inert mass. I will repeat this act only because you requested me to provide you with an energy source to prolong your own lives."

"I'm so sorry." Toby apologized for their need to eat. "Would killing rabbits be easier for you?"

Orvis considered that alternative. "No."

"How about insects? Or snakes?" said Thaddeus.

"No. But if you need to consume them, I will kill them." Orvis's lights blinked in almost full thinking array. "What I do not yet understand is how humans justify the logic of causing death when food is not the objective."

"I guess they just don't think about it too much," said Thaddeus.

Orvis did not reply.

Toby picked up one of the pheasants and cradled it in her hands, surprised by its lightness. Feathers made birds look much bigger than they were. The bird's eyes were shut, the soft gray craped lid relaxed, as if the hen slept. She smoothed the neck feathers, watching the light play over the intricate markings, hating what she had to do. How had people managed to live this way so long?

"Janet Frome's *Book of Ancient Cookery* states the bird's

head must be removed and the blood allowed to drain," Orvis informed her.

Thaddeus moaned softly. "Do I have to?"

Toby began to imagine how the birds would cook if that step was omitted but the idea was too unpleasant. "What else did the book say, Orvis?"

As he gave them the details of how to dress a bird she began to feel faint. Did the man who was the butcher at the Academy have to do this all the time? Or the cooks? No wonder people moved away from Earth and switched to synthetic foods. She wanted to curl up under the tree and go to sleep, to never have to think again about what had to be done to keep alive out here. She was so tired, and the idea of endless sleep was so inviting that it frightened her.

"Don't think about it, Thaddeus," she said. "If we do, we'll starve to death. We'll just do what we have to. You take the feathers off one and I'll do the other."

With Orvis's instructions and the glass shard for a knife, they managed. More than an hour passed before the pheasants were ready to be spitted. By that time both birds and children looked much the worse for wear.

Leaving Orvis to turn the spit, they went to wash in the creek. She scrubbed her hands with sand until they tingled but her fingers still smelled of raw poultry.

"Is this a character-building experience?" Thaddeus was kneeling on a rock, cleaning his nails with a split twig. "When we have to do something hard in physical therapy or gym, the coach says it's 'character-building.' "

"I'm not even sure what that means," she said. "I think it's one of those things grown-ups say when they're sick of hearing kids complain."

The creek was full of watercress but neither recognized the plant as edible. Toby gathered some dandelions and washed them, not because she wanted to but because habit suggested they should have vegetables. By sundown the roasting birds smelled and looked like food; Orvis took their temperature and pronounced them cooked.

"Real meat tastes funny and it's tough." Thaddeus's right cheek was bulging as he laboriously chewed a bite of drumstick into a wad soft enough to risk swallowing. "I mean, even at school, it doesn't have much taste and what it has isn't good. I remember, when I was a little kid, I liked the meat on shipboard."

"This needs salt, that's all." Toby was trying to make the best of a meal she wasn't enjoying either. "And it's tough because it's wild. With flying and all, birds exercise a lot." Her nose wrinkled with distaste as she peered at the white meat in her hand, then gingerly picked off a cooked pinfeather and several ribs and flicked them into the fire. "You want some salad?" She held out a dandelion leaf.

"No thanks." His throat bulged as he managed to swallow the bolus of meat he'd been chewing. "Why do you think real food tastes like this? I mean, it's much more expensive, so it should taste better."

"Ask Orvis," Toby suggested.

"Humans are born neophobic about food—meaning they dislike any new taste. Children adopt the food preferences of their prime nurturer or parent," said Orvis. "According to Charlotte Huehngarth, Ph.D., in her study *Satisfying Ex-Terran Tastes and Nutritional Needs*, humans are born with a taste preference for sweet and an aversion to bitterness. This is due to primitive human feeding habits in the wild, where sweet plants were nutritious and bitter plants were often poisonous."

Toby quickly spit out the bitter dandelion leaf she was munching rabbitlike.

"As early as the twentieth century," Orvis went on, "biochemists, flavorists, and psychologists employed by the food and chemical industries had learned to isolate the chemical compounds specific to a flavor—that of blueberries, for example. By artificially duplicating and compounding that flavor they could make a synthetic fruit nugget that tasted more like blueberry than any real blueberry could."

Toby frowned. "How does all that answer our question?"

"Foodstuffs on space ships and in most habitats are by necessity synthetic. Your taste buds were initially programmed to accept artificially flavored synthetic foods—food with more taste than that grown naturally. All natural foods will taste *new* to you, lacking the degree of flavor and salts you have been programmed to accept as *appetizing*."

"Oh." Thaddeus thought it over. "That makes sense."

"But why didn't people just stick with real food?" said Toby.

"Are you asking me?" said Orvis.

"Yes."

"Aside from its unavailability—are you prepared to wait while I search and summarize more than two hundred data hours of input regarding human nutrition?"

"No. I'm not *that* interested." She grinned at the robot and then felt silly. *Humans smile to avert threat.* "Maybe you could just run samples of what we can find here to eat through your chromatograph and let us know if anything is poisonous?"

"I have already done that. The dandelion is not poisonous."

"Let's save the other bird for breakfast. Okay?" said Thaddeus.

The fire warmed the cement beneath the logs. After brushing away pebbles they stretched out on the pavement, too tired to worry about the hardness of their bed. And, as Thaddeus pointed out, on the pale gray cement they could see big bugs or snakes coming toward them even in the dark. She wished he hadn't shared that thought with her.

"Before you came to Earth, did you know there were so many stars?" he asked, staring up at the sky.

"No. You can't see them from inside the habitats unless you go to the sky observation lounges. And if you're under ten years old, you can't go in there."

"Why?"

"The little kids get scared. They think the windows might open and they'd never stop falling."

"They wouldn't fall far," he said. "They'd orbit the colony, like little moons held close by gravity."

"Why don't you go tell them that? It would make them feel much better."

He ignored her sarcasm. "On the ship you can only see the stars on the screen, so you never see more than six square feet of sky, and sometimes the screen just looks black if you're passing through an empty area. There aren't any windows."

"Didn't it bother you, being shut in like that?"

"No. I didn't know anything else. Until I came to Earth I never even thought about windows to the outside. They scared me at first; I was afraid things could get in at you when you were sleeping."

"Things like what?"

"Oh . . . Bad people. Snakes. Wild animals. Like that."

"Does it still scare you?"

"Yes," he admitted, "but out here it's so scary that, if we make it, I don't think much else will scare me again."

"We'll make it," she said, and tried to tell herself it was true.

After he fell asleep she lay watching the new moon set, then tried to count the satellites in their swift passage across the sky. Her parents and Lillian were up there, somewhere—warm, safe, and comfortable. Did they know she was lost? If so, the school was in trouble. Not that it mattered; the Academy seemed as distant now as any habitat, and as impossible to reach. Reality was this: the fire, the tree branches overhead, having to eat wild things, being stalked by a cougar, and the reassuring squeak of the damaged leg of an ancient robot who stood guard over them.

A light wind brushed the trees and made the fire smoke and glow. She shivered in her light jacket and moved closer to Thaddeus. Both dozed fitfully, like animals, waking at every strange sound and scent.

TEN

Orvis put a pine stump in the center of the fire. As he stepped back from the flames a strip of burning bark clung to his front toes. Sparks flared with each step until the bark curled and shriveled away to ashes.

A stranger coming on the scene would have been horrified to see this mechanical thing looming over the sleeping children, its camera eyes gleaming blue in the firelight. A small panel on its belly opened; a thing resembling a suede flyswatter flexed down and hovered first over Toby, and then over Thaddeus. It touched each forehead, throat, and hand. A series of tiny multicolored lights blinked on and off before the tool retracted and a frontal amber light came on. Then, abruptly, the robot backed away and walked into the night.

As he walked Orvis analyzed the data gained from the vitascan: the surface temperature of their housing was too low; the pump circulating the liquids in their system should not be working at such high speed while they were at rest; their exhaust was slightly toxic, indicating inadequate or incomplete fuel combustion. In the event of rain or undue cold they might cease to function.

A cold breeze woke Toby. Her watch said 3:15. She'd been dreaming of a choir singing and for a moment lay puzzling as to why she'd been dreaming that. Thaddeus lay curled against her, one arm flung over her waist like a weight to keep her close in case she tried to leave him. His head was pillowed on her left arm and her hand was so numb that her fingers felt like dead nubbins when she tried to wiggle them.

Odd, she thought, wondering both at his trusting closeness and her own comfort in his closeness. Then as gently as possible she began to free herself. Thaddeus's eyelids fluttered and he tried to hug her closer. "I have to go to the bathroom," she whispered. He grunted in reluctant consent and moved away, allowing her to sit up. The air felt cold against her back.

Rubbing circulation back into her arm, she stared into the fire. Flames were curling over the roots and licking up the hollow inside of the stump. The juice of insects buried in the bark sang as it gasified and the gases popped in tiny explosions of blue and green flames. A dog barked in the distance. Another answered from farther away. Wild dogs? She shivered at the thought and looked around for Orvis.

"There is a habitation." His voice came from the darkness behind her.

"Where?" she whispered, scrambling to her feet.

"West northwest by twelve degrees."

Where the moon set, she reminded herself, trying not to get excited or to hope. She failed in both. "I don't see any light."

"There are no lights. There are buildings. They are occupied. I have analyzed the heat waves rising from them."

She made her way through the wet grass and briars to where he stood. No matter how she tried, she could see nothing but the dark outline of trees against the horizon.

"Are you sure?"

"Yes. Two of my lenses are light-intensifying. Two see infrared."

"Can you see people?"

"No. I hear voices. They are singing. I also hear dogs and other animals."

"What are you two talking about? You woke me." Thaddeus sounded grumpy as he stumbled through the grass to join them.

An hour later the three of them stood on a slope overlooking a walled village; its buildings glistened like snow under the starlight. In the center of the village was a wide plaza, bordered on one side by a large oval building with a domed tower and a courtyard. Oblong structures flanked both ends of the square. Across from the tower was a cluster of small half-spheres, like the solar domes of individual houses. To the west, but still inside the walls, was a multispired structure, several large tanks, and a hydrogen gas tank that looked like a huge silver ball.

"There are approximately one hundred people singing in the courtyard," said Orvis. "They are standing in rows, looking up at the sky."

"It sounds like a religious song," Thaddeus whispered. The voices were well-trained, the sound clear and true.

"It's part of an opera," Toby said. She smiled as she recalled the hours of screen background music her parents stole from operas.

"*Flight Through the Rings of Nardos*, by Ian McCall," said Orvis. "The opera was first performed by the Seattle Opera Company on January 12, 2235. Do you wish to hear the critical reception?"

"No," said Toby.

"The critics found it lush and sentimental."

Toby giggled in spite of their situation. "And it's only lasted three hundred years," she said. "I wonder how long it would last if they'd liked it?"

A breeze brushed around them, carrying a distinct barnyard smell. Several dogs began to bark, but without urgency. Briar scratches on Toby's ankles itched and she scratched them with the toes of her boots. Her pants legs were wet from the grass and she was shivering.

"Let's see if we can get inside. I'm cold."

"There is a gate to the right of this position. An unpaved roadway leads from the gate to this orchard," Orvis quietly informed them.

"How do you know we're in an orchard?" All she'd seen were medium-sized trees in the dark.

"Tended trees, geometrically spaced. The scent of fertilizer and apple blossoms," said Orvis.

At the edge of the orchard were clear plastic structures that glinted like greenhouses in the night. Beyond, a bridge crossed a stream shallow enough to babble over the stones in its bed. Their boots crunched into gravel and Orvis's metal toes rang like rake tines through the pebbles.

"You'd think they'd put lights out here. Or at least a security guard," Thaddeus complained in a whisper as they approached the gate.

"But there's no one else around for miles."

"We are."

"Only by accident."

A dog began to bark on the other side of the wall. Several more quickly joined in. "Stop right there!" a man's voice called. "Who are you? What do you want here?" The accent was strange, almost foreign, and hostile.

"Two men are observing us from the top of the wall," said Orvis.

All she could see were two vague blurs, one slightly higher than the other. "Hello?" she called. "We're lost. Could you help us, please?" In the silence they could hear the creek gurgling behind them, the singing in the distance.

"Maybe they're deaf?" suggested Thaddeus.

"Hello?" she called more loudly. The dogs barked louder, too. "I'm Toby West. This is Thaddeus Hall. And that's Orvis—he's a robot." She paused again, then blithered nervously. "We were on our way to see my great-grandmother at Fisher's Isle. Our pilot answered an SOS and the two men he came to help stole his truck and kidnapped him to help fly it and they left us out here. We thought an air patrol car would come along but none did. You're the first people we've seen in two days."

The sympathetic response she expected still did not come. "Could we use your phone? Please? Or could you call for help?"

After a dismayingly long silence the larger of the two blurs leaned closer to the other and spoke. He made no attempt to keep from being overheard but although Toby listened closely the few words she could understand made no sense to her.

"Shupp!" one of them shouted and the barking stopped.

"Say all that over. What you said. Slow," the shorter blur called. He spoke very slowly and much too loudly, as if he thought they were deaf.

When Toby had done as ordered, and repeated everything twice after that, the two men again discussed the situation among themselves. But now she understood two words: "kid" and "robot."

"There's just you two and the robot?" one asked, as if to confirm the other's question.

"Yes, sir," Thaddeus spoke up. "We've come a long way and we're cold and tired and hungry. Please, can't we come inside?"

"You're children? Real children?"

"Yes, sir . . ." What did he think they were?

After more discussion they decided: "You come in. The robot stays out for now. You understand?"

"Yes, sir," said Thaddeus.

"Will the robot be safe out here?" Toby asked. "My great-grandmother is looking forward to seeing him and—"

"Who's to bother it?" one of them asked. A dim red light came on over the gate and made the night seem darker and more frightening.

She hesitated but Thaddeus's teeth were beginning to chatter. "You go and hide," she whispered to Orvis. "But don't go too far. Help should be here soon now."

"Yes," said Orvis. But it would not be help for him.

The gate slid open on tracks that screeched with dust and grit. Metal gleamed as the men came down steps inside the wall to meet them. Both were carrying stubby guns with nightsights. Since Toby's first impression was that neither man was too bright, the idea of their being armed was more frightening.

"How did you find us?" the tall one asked in his slow way.

"We heard the music."

"Was it the Johnson brothers stole your truck?"

"They didn't introduce themselves," said Thaddeus in all seriousness.

"Who are the Johnson brothers and what do they look like?" she asked, wondering what possible difference this could make at the moment.

"Criminals. They live out there. Somewhere. They came here twice. Stole pigs. That's why we got the dogs. To warn us. They fly junked trucks."

"Whole family. Live out there in The Empty," volunteered the other man.

"Are the Johnsons dirty? And tall and thin?" asked Toby.

"And talk dirty?" remembered Thaddeus.

"Sounds like them," said the self-appointed leader and the two men nodded to each other.

"Maybe we should tell that to the air patrol when we call them now?" Toby said, trying to get the conversation back to using the phone. "That it was them?"

"No," said the short one.

"You have to see Mr. Milton," the taller one said. "The Commander."

"Is this a military post?"

"No. Mr. Milton's busy now," said the other. "You have to wait."

"Can't we call for help while we wait to see him?" asked Toby.

"No."

"Could you please call the police for us?"

Thaddeus's question was ignored. The gate closed behind them, shutting Orvis out and shutting them inside. The red light over the gate went off.

There was a grove of trees inside the gate and what appeared to be thick-walled pens which stank of manure. A pig woke to question their footsteps with a fleshy snuffle. The barnyard smells were left behind, gravel gave way to pavement, but there were still no lights. When Thaddeus asked why he was told, "So we can see the stars."

"Oh."

"What's the name of this town?" asked Toby.

"No name."

"How can we tell people where to find us?"

"Don't worry about it."

Toby was not sure coming here was a good idea; she was getting more frightened by the minute. She suddenly recalled how Terrans once housed the mentally ill in isolated places. That might explain this odd pair, and the strange singing in the middle of the night. Music might be part of their therapy, along with caring for animals. But if this was a hospital, where were the doctors, the guards . . . ?

"Wait in there."

Orvis scaled the wall with insect-ease, legs outstretched, toes gripping minute indentations. His climbing technique had been perfected by his careful observation of spiders and grasshoppers as they walked up sheer cliff walls.

With age and experience the old robot had come to regret a certain lack of plasticity in his design, one of the imperfections he was thus far unable to correct and constantly had to compensate for. For one thing, his body did not bend. Lacking segmentation, he was unable to loop over this wall and walk down. This awkwardness caused him to reach the ground rear end first so that he had to back away on toetips, without the use of his forelegs. While this system was adequate, it was also jarring.

With all six legs firmly on the ground again, he folded the defective pair to eliminate their screeching. By the time he had regained both poise and balance, the children and their escorts were out of sight and hearing. A panel opened on his back, a rod pushed up, and plates unfurled into a dish antenna that tipped and turned, scanning until locking on the sound of footsteps. Four individuals, two large, two small. Orvis moved off into the darkened village.

He had gone a quarter mile when the dogs discovered him and came running, barking with excitement. He had to stop and think. Stunning would silence them but would cause enmity. Humans were peculiar about their live possessions. Pain or fear left no marks. When he emitted sounds above the range of human hearing the unfortunate dogs fell over one another in their haste to get away.

Halting in deep shadow, he watched the children enter the silo structure. One man hurried back toward the gate; the other entered the building where the choir sang. Seeing a tangle of shrubbery between the silo tower and the building with the courtyard, Orvis hid behind the bushes, next to the wall. He could hear them inside, calling to each other, walking about.

With the smallest of his lasers he silently cut through the wall and inserted a flexlens fiber into the hole. "We have visual," he confirmed to himself out of habit. The room was dimly lit. They were sitting on an upholstered bench that circled half the wall. They looked small and intimidated. Arching over a second door a ramp led up to another floor, where the base of an obsolete telescope was visible. An amateur astronomical observatory.

ELEVEN

Maybe they think we don't have credit because we're young? That's why we have to get special permission to phone? So they don't have to pay for the call?"

"You think they're that cheap?" Thaddeus kicked off his boots and tucked his feet beneath him to try to get them warm.

"Or that poor."

"We could tell them how much credit we have."

"Lillian says *never* to do that. People try to take advantage of you if they know you're rich. Especially if you're a kid."

"Oh." He puzzled over that and then his face brightened as he thought of the solution: "We'll call collect."

"Why do *we* have to call?" she wondered. "If two lost kids turned up at the Academy, for example, the first person they met would run to call the authorities. Why don't they do that here?"

"I don't know—but I've never been lost before."

In the silence they could hear the choir in the courtyard next door. The tower acted as a muffling sound chamber, softening the voices, blurring them. The music, combined with getting warm again, made them sleepy. When the door under the ramp opened suddenly, both jumped to their feet.

The man who stood there wore sandals, a white tunic that came to his knees, and a belt that made him look like a flour sack tied in the middle. His cheeks were red and shiny, as was the top of his head. His dark eyes were fever bright. Frizzles of gray hair bunched over his ears. After studying them for a moment he came into the room and carefully seated himself on the round bench in the center, crossed his knees, clasped his hands over the right knee, and smiled at them.

"Don't you think—this isn't meant as criticism, or inspired by envy because I myself have reached the point where my system can't tolerate further rejuvenation—but don't you think you're overdoing the youth treatments? I mean, you must forgive my frankness, but you both look like children."

"We are children," said Thaddeus, frowning. Toby simply stared at the man, sure her theory about this being a mental hospital was correct.

"Children? Really! How marvelous! I couldn't quite understand Leon. The music, you know. I gathered you were man and wife, left stranded by hijackers."

"Are you Mr. Milton?" asked Toby, unsure if he was teasing them or simply crazy. He was staring so intently. "You're the Commander?"

"I was," he said, then added in a bemused tone, "I believe you *are* children. Amazing!"

"May we please use a vu-phone? The men at the gate said we had to ask your permission. People will be worried about us. We've been lost for two days."

His smile turned rueful. "I'm sorry. We have no phone."

"Please don't tease us. We just want—"

"I'm not teasing. We have no vu-phone."

She and Thaddeus exchanged glances of fear and disbelief. "Don't you even have a radio?" said Thaddeus.

"I'm afraid not." He smiled apologetically and recrossed his knees. "We are a sequestered community."

"What does that mean?"

"Voluntarily isolated from the world."

"What do you do in emergencies?"

"What we've always done. Handle them ourselves."

He paused and drew a breath as a teacher might before beginning a difficult lesson. "All of us here, from crew to officers, are accustomed to isolation. We have spent our lives—our whole careers—in deep space, either in ships or research stations, in places so distant that message transmission sometimes took years to reach Earth. When our duty tours ended and we returned here for retirement and reorientation, we didn't know a soul on Earth. No one knew us. Only the computers remembered who we were, where we had been, and why. And they didn't care either. We left Earth believing we were the Future. We came back to find we were the long-forgotten Past."

Thaddeus leaned forward in rapt attention.

"Our memories of Earth," Mr. Milton went on, "the customs, even the language—as you have no doubt noticed—were sadly out-of-date. At the Lakeside Reorientation Center some of us got together in our loneliness and pooled our knowledge and savings and beliefs, and we built a place for ourselves. That was twenty years ago. As aliens on our own world, we chose the most isolated area we could find. Anything we have to say to people now isn't something they want to hear. For us there is no place like home."

"Why didn't you go live in a habitat?" said Toby.

"We're from Earth. And we had all had enough of simulation. We were born here; Earth was what we dreamed of returning to. Only society had changed—so we have made our own society."

"My parents re-enlisted," said Thaddeus. "They were too lonely here."

"They must still be young." For the first time the man's glance met the boy's.

"Yes, sir." Thaddeus had never thought of them as young, but compared to this man they were.

"You were born here?" the man asked.

"No. In space. On their return trip."

"Really? They've relaxed the rules. I keep forgetting. No

babies were allowed in our time. And they came back and left you here?"

Thaddeus nodded yes.

"Sensible. And you?" This question was directed at Toby.

"In the Greenhouse habitat in—Please, can't we talk later? Or are you saying you won't help us at all?"

"No. No!" He seemed startled that he'd given her that impression. "Of course we'll help you. I was just coming to that. You must excuse me. I haven't spoken with a child in I don't know how long. Or with any outsider in weeks, for that matter. We do have a shuttle, an air taxi, whatever today's civilians call them. When we have to, we can fly over to the city on the lake for supplies." His smile didn't quite take in his too-bright eyes.

"The taxi has a radio!" But Toby's relief at that thought was promptly squashed.

"Yes, normally." His smile faded to regret. "But it's in the repair bay now. The shuttle. Something wrong with the fuel cell, and the electrical system. But we'll repair it," he said, brightening.

"How long will that take?" asked Thaddeus.

"We were in no rush. I can find out. In the meantime, you'll be our guests. You'll be quite safe here. And we're delighted to have you."

"Maybe we should just stay till morning and go on with Orvis," Toby said to Thaddeus. "We could be at Fisher's Isle by the time—"

"I don't think that's wise at all." Mr. Milton spoke before

Thaddeus could answer. "Even if we gave you food and warmer clothing, there are all sorts of predators out there, both animal and human. As you know all too well or you wouldn't be sitting here talking with me. No, I wouldn't feel at all right letting you leave."

"Does anyone ever get to leave here?" Thaddeus was obviously scared.

"Of course." The benign smile returned, then faded again. "We can leave anytime we wish, normally. Of course, most of us don't want to. When you stay in one place too long, change is terrifying. Now!" He clapped his hands together and stood up. "Let's find you a place to sleep. I should think the Olaf place will do. That's still empty."

After the warmth of the tower the air outside felt cold and damp and the night seemed darker. Twice when the singing went soft enough Toby was sure she heard Orvis, but when she turned around to see, he wasn't there. It was odd how, once you got used to hearing a sound, you went on hearing it even after it stopped. Dogs began barking again and then the barking changed to yips and frightened whines as if the animals had been cuffed. Mr. Milton paid no attention but went on with his rambling village history.

Why don't I believe him? Toby wondered. Because he never smiles with his eyes? Because having the fuel cell out is too convenient? It could be true. Because he never stops talking? Or because he looks so odd? But then maybe we look odd to him, and maybe children make him nervous, too, if there aren't any here.

They were walking along a real sidewalk now, with houses to the right and what appeared to be a park on the other side. She could see branches against the night sky. Each house stood alone on its own lot, squares with domes on top, each with an arched doorway and a round window to the left of the door. All the lights were out, as if everyone were in bed. She had never seen separate houses before and wondered why they had been built that way, especially here, where winter came.

"Why are people outside singing at this time of night?" she heard Thaddeus ask.

"Because the stars are most visible now. We sing devotions each clear night from three until dawn."

"Oh."

"You must believe in something, son. Otherwise, what is it all for?"

"You worship the stars? Why?"

"Why not? All life came from the stars. We're made up of their atoms. In time we return to star dust. Eons after our intelligence, the pure light of our energy, has rejoined the Higher Intelligence. Here we believe we are all part of the Higher Intelligence that is the Universe. Cells within cells within cells. Stars beyond stars . . . Are you a true believer?"

"I don't think so, sir." Thaddeus lagged behind and caught her hand for reassurance. "I don't really understand what you just said."

"Pity. When you can understand and believe you're

much less frightened when you're lost. Belief would comfort you now. Far more than we can."

"I don't think so," Thaddeus said thoughtfully. "I mean, our sun is a star—like other stars—and I can't believe it could care one way or the other what happens to me."

"That's because your thinking is still encapsulated, still bounded by the personal, the 'Me,' but when you have grasped that you are truly star dust, truly part of the Universe, you will see how *caring* limits you. Then you will know you are infinite, immortal."

It's because I'm tired that he frightens me, Toby decided. If we were at school I'd just tell myself he was a little crazy and not listen.

"Wait here."

The man stopped beside the entrance to one of the houses. "I have to make sure the blinds are closed. Lights distract their focus. They would never forgive us." He stepped back from the door and stood with his chin tilted, smiling up at the haze of the Milky Way. "Look up there! Did you ever see anything so magnificent? We were there. So many times. And we'll be there again. Light-years away. Light-years from now. Soon!"

His final sigh was echoed by the door as he let himself into the darkened house and the door closed.

"After listening to him, I guess I can understand better why my parents went away again," Thaddeus said as they waited on the doorstep. "But he does seem a little strange," he added.

"Maybe that's where the term 'spaced-out' comes from?"

she whispered. "I read that old-time spacers got brain dam-age from radiation. A cell got bombarded here and there, till after a while their brains were shot through like lace. The rest of their bodies got damaged, too, and they—"

"My parents weren't spaced out," Thaddeus said indig-nantly.

"I didn't say they were. But they're a lot younger than this man. Besides, the ships now have better hull shielding against radiation than when he probably started out. How old do you think he—"

The door hissed open again and they automatically stepped back. Mr. Milton was an upright white oblong in the shadows of the entry. "Come in," he said. "I've turned the house on. Lighting will activate in two minutes. I must get back to the church. I'll have the kitchen send over some food after the services, so don't lock your doors."

"Yes, sir."

"Thank you very much," Toby said as he brushed past.

On the doorstep he turned to give them one last order. "You must respect our no-light rules. Keep the blinds closed until sunup."

"Yes, sir."

They felt their way into the strange building, smelling its unfamiliar odors, touching the walls for guidance until the front door closed and the lights came on.

"It's like a space-ship cabin!" Thaddeus smiled with pleasure as he stepped down into the small living room. "But with windows and no console."

The walls and ceiling glowed with daybrite. Red and

golden iridescent lightballs floated like huge soap bubbles.
The furnishings were foam-formed, in colors ranging from
beige to peach to lavender, the seating cushioned in what
looked like frosty velvet. A tropical-fish biosphere glowed
in the corner; its occupants appeared unsurprised to have
company again. Through an archway was a short hall leading to a utility room. A ramp over the arch led to four
closet-sized rooms, all identical with a recessed airbed,
desk, chair, and storage locker. Two bathrooms filled the
building core.

In one of the drawers in the room Toby chose she found
a stack of adult clothing, including tunics, worn but clean
and neatly folded.

"Here." She handed a yellow shirt to Thaddeus and kept
a white one for herself. "Our clothes are too filthy to put
back on after we shower."

He made a face but took the shirt. "If they were so tired
of space, why do you think they made their houses look
like this?" he asked.

"Maybe this was the only kind of room they could feel
at home in now?"

"Maybe."

When she undressed she found a large bruise where the
man had kicked her—purple-yellow and sore to the touch.
The scrape on her knee was scabby and the weed scratch
on her ankle was red and puckered but healing. She
couldn't remember appreciating toilet tissue before, or
soap, or hot water, things she'd always taken as much for
granted as breathing. Lacking a proper nail brush, she

washed her hair three times just to get her nails clean again, and then combed her hair with the luxury of a real comb. To use the tooth-jet and put on something clean and dry was almost as nice as stretching out on the bed cushion and feeling its heater come on. She sighed with pleasure at being warm again, and indoors, and having some privacy. Much as she liked Thaddeus, forty-eight hours together was a little long. Reaching out to pull the cover over her, she sneezed.

"Do you believe they don't have any way to talk with outsiders?" Thaddeus called from his bed. He sounded lonesome.

"I don't know. What if . . ." She considered sharing her theory that this might be a mental hospital or colony, then decided not to. It wasn't the sort of thought one wanted to go to sleep on. "Maybe the man is teasing us and will surprise us in the morning by having a patrol car here to take us home."

"Maybe. But what if he doesn't? Or isn't?"

"We'll find out in the morning," she said.

"Do you think he was a ship's officer?"

"He sounds like one."

"Why do you think he dresses like that?"

"Maybe they sing to the stars in their nightclothes?" she said.

Thaddeus giggled. "They must get cold."

Toby thought about wearing sandals and a tunic in the cold, as she slowly drifted into dreams—dreams of them still walking. Had she stayed awake half a minute more she would have heard Thaddeus's first snore.

In the gray of early dawn a woman carrying an insulated hot tray opened the front door and paused to listen before entering. After setting the tray on a table in the living room, she tiptoed up the ramp and looked in on each of them. When she left, she took their discarded clothing and boots with her.

No sooner had she gone than the rear door opened and Orvis entered the utility room. He paused to survey the equipment in the space, assured himself of clearance, and walked into the main room. Using a forefoot as tongs, he removed the top of the tray and took inventory. Four chicken eggs heated to a solid state, buttered bread, stewed apples, two empty mugs, a squat container full of cow's milk. From his underbelly a tube snaked down and the tip penetrated each foodstuff, like a butterfly's proboscis testing nectar. A minute sample was siphoned into the gasification chamber for analysis. All was found safe for human consumption, although the milk contained bacteria. One minute of radiation killed all living organisms in the liquid.

After replacing the lid he climbed the narrow ramp. The upper hall was too curved to permit his entry. Doing an analytic scan from where he stood he satisfied himself that the children's condition was improved by heat and shelter, then backed down the ramp and returned to the utility room.

There was a shelf in that room on which he'd seen a stack of toweling and several cans of lubricant. Below the shelf was a sink. Orvis set to work cleaning himself. He was still engaged in polishing when the first of the gift bearers arrived an hour after dawn.

For several hours they came alone or in pairs, entering the house as quietly as people enter a shrine. When the tabletops were covered with offerings they put their gifts on the sofa, then draped garments over the lounges and chairs. Flowers were brought, and fruit in bowls and baskets crudely woven of grass. They left as quietly as they came, except for one old man who cried out in pleased surprise when he saw Orvis through the archway. "I remember bots like you! Boy, once we were both state-of-the-art! Good to see you, fellow!"

"Do not wake Toby and Thaddeus," said Orvis.

It was his voice that woke Toby.

TWELVE

Daylight rimmed the blind Toby opened. The sky, so clear before, was now gray with clouds. Beyond the raindrops on the dirty window a maple branch shivered in the wind. She stared up at the new leaves, depressed as much by low blood sugar as by disappointment in remembering where she was.

All this was for nothing. Orvis was still a fugitive. Because he was her friend, Thaddeus was in danger. Even if they reached Goldie's place, the people at the Academy or Lillian and her parents would make sure there wasn't time to visit and get to know her great-grandmother. Or convince the woman to give Orvis a home. It was like a dumb screen game: "Whoops! You lose. Go directly to Mars."

In spite of herself she grinned; the game wasn't over—she might win yet. Unless she gave up, and she wasn't going to do that. Besides, it was morning and she'd always

liked Earth mornings—they offered hope, not just a change
in light level.

The view from the window wasn't encouraging—trees
and the rear of other houses like this one. One thing she
had noticed about Earth-borns; they weren't neat about
their surroundings. But then they had room enough to be
untidy. Directly below was an unkempt lawn where two
brown-and-white goats grazed and twitched their ears
against the drizzle. One of the goats said *"Maal,"* the other
chewed a daffodil. That flower eaten, the goat nosed the
ground, eager to complete the ruin of a flower bed. There
was a pile of building rubble behind the goats. Brush grew
through a rusting scrap pile. A ditch in the lawn had never
been filled in; pipes lay exposed beneath rain-dimpled water.

The more she looked, the shabbier the place seemed. As
if nothing was ever picked up and put away, but just left
where it had been used last. On impulse she turned and
looked around her room. At night, and tired, she hadn't
noticed that in the color scheme of dusty rose and brown,
the dust was real and thick. But didn't they have cleaning
rovers?

"Boo!" At Thaddeus's harsh whisper she jumped so high
her head struck the padded roof of the bed. "I'm sorry," he
said but he giggled. "I didn't mean to scare you *that* much.
Did you hear a noise in the living room?"

"I don't know. Maybe that's what woke me." She rubbed
her head and moved over as he knelt on her bed to look
out the window.

"Should we go down and see?" he asked.

"After we find some other clothes." For the first time she saw that the yellow tunic fit him like a sack, the shoulders down to his elbows, the sleeves a foot too long. The hem that dragged the floor was full of dust-kittens.

"You don't look too wonderful yourself, you know," he said, guessing what she was thinking by her expression.

"Maybe we can buy some clothes? If—"

Both fell silent at the sound of the front door opening and closing. Footsteps crossed the floor below; pillows sighed as if being sat on. There were furtive rustling sounds, and then the door opened and closed again.

"Did they leave?"

"I'd go down but I don't want anybody to see me like this," he said.

"I'll go. I'm not proud." She spoke with more confidence than she felt. At the top of the ramp she paused to finger-comb her hair and smooth the nightshirt to make herself more presentable, took a deep breath, and started down. She couldn't hear anyone, but the air in the house smelled of wet clothing and some sort of cleaning agent.

"Orvis!" She was so glad to see him at the foot of the ramp that she could have hugged him, had that been possible without getting poked by his protuberances. "Orvis is here!" she called, adding after a quick glance around, "and nobody else." She pushed past Orvis and went to lock the front door for privacy. "How did you get here?" she asked the robot as Thaddeus came running down.

"Access to the enclosure was as easy as it is incidental,"

said Orvis. "You have had visitors. One brought food. The others brought inedibles. None expressed hostility toward myself and one expressed recognition of my ancient genre."

"What does that mean?"

"He was glad to see me."

"Mr. Milton spoke in error," Orvis informed them as they cracked and peeled their eggs. "This colony has five aircraft: two one-ton utility vans, one five-ton cargo van, two ten-passenger cars. All lack fuel cells and communication equipment but otherwise appear operable."

"Did they take the fuel cells and stuff out on purpose?" said Toby, and then had to explain what "on purpose" meant.

"Why would they do that?" said Thaddeus.

"I don't know," Toby and Orvis said in unison and she giggled as Orvis continued. "Mr. Milton also erred in saying repairs were in progress. There is no sign of repairs. There is no sign of repairs being needed, other than replacement of the missing equipment."

Toby stopped chewing and stared down at the greenish coating on the egg yolk. Had Mr. Milton lied to them about everything? Thaddeus was looking at her, the same concern reflected on his face. Absently, they both began to examine their gifts.

"Do you think we should get out of here?" he said.

"As soon as we can!"

"They'll probably try to stop us. Mr. Milton said it was too dangerous for us to go out alone. But I think we should explore the village, find out where the gates are, and where we can get food, and blankets."

"We can do that today, after it stops raining," she said. "Why would they want to keep us here?"

"Maybe they don't and we're just imagining things?" said Thaddeus. Toby nodded in half-hearted agreement. But neither was convinced of that.

"Why would someone I've never met give me an emerald-and-diamond bracelet?" was Toby's next question. She held the band of brilliants to the light and watched them sparkle. "Even if I could accept it, I couldn't wear it. Not until I'm grown up. My mother would say 'vulgar' in that voice of hers . . ." She carefully fitted the bracelet back into its velvet box.

"Why would she say that? It's pretty . . ." Thaddeus's voice faded as he opened a box marked "For the boy" and found inside a jeweled commemorative belt. "Wow!" With a forefinger he traced out the pavé diamond letters: *Uranus Expedition, 2235*. "Why would someone give that away? They don't even know me."

"Here's a ring. And a necklace. And a . . . something." She held up a rod of crystal that hummed. "It's all beautiful, but what's it for?"

They watched as Orvis neatly removed the necklace from its worn black velvet case. "The necklace is very fine," he said, scrutinizing it as it dangled from his right front toes. "I would judge twentieth century. The mounting is eighteen karat gold . . . Italian work. The rubies are a matched suite, natural, probably Burmese. It needs cleaning." He refitted

the piece into its molded hollow and closed the case with
a snap. "The antique dealer who owned me taught me to
assist in appraisals—though I was also part of the inventory. The pavé diamond belt has little resale value, except
to a collector of space memorabilia. These items appear to
be heirlooms—precious human possessions passed on to
the generation to follow. A community with no living de-
scendants and no antique dealers would have problems in
disposing of heirlooms. You are apparently their benefici-
aries."

"You mean, if they had children, they would have given
these things to them, but since they didn't—" Thaddeus
considered the idea and then looked at the belt again.
"That's very sad."

"Yes," Toby agreed. "Also, a little scary."

In the quiet of the room they became aware of muted
voices in the street outside, as if a crowd had gathered. Just
then someone tried to open the door and both of them froze
until the footsteps went away. Toby glanced at the time; it
was just after noon.

"Maybe we should get dressed and go out before they
force their way in? Or start to worry," she added, seeing
the idea made him nervous.

"I guess so."

The gifts of clothing were their size, obviously home-
made, and looked as if they had been cut from old dress
uniforms. The fabrics were elegant and sturdy, if slightly
musty. They found themselves unfolding blue, white, and
lemon-yellow jackets, satiny tunics with the metallic sheen

of gold, silver, or black shot with glo-fiber, and matte-finished pants. Toby found one tunic of dark blue that flashed with blue-green opalescence like a tropical sea at night.

"This looks as if they raided the studio wardrobe department." She held the blouse up for Thaddeus to admire. "Isn't it beautiful? If I were thirty . . . I always wanted to be thirty."

"Thirty's nice," he said agreeably, more interested in a pair of white boots. "Why would your studio have clothing like this?"

"For historical or period films."

"Oh." He thought that over. "I like this stuff." With that he gathered up the garments tagged with his name. "I'm going up and try them on. Want to?"

In spite of being worried about people at their door, they spent almost an hour trying on all the clothes and running in and out of their rooms to show each other how an outfit looked before finally choosing what they would wear.

"Look at me, Orvis," Thaddeus said, admiring himself in a mirrored wall. "What do you think?"

"You are pretty," said Orvis.

"Handsome," corrected Toby, and grinned at her own reflection of blue satin, silver, and white, thinking how her mother would loathe the flash of it.

"Pretty," insisted Orvis. "Anyone dressed in a yellow jacket, gold shirt, and tight ivory pants is pretty. 'Handsome' would indicate more restraint."

"I'm glad the kids at school can't see me," said Thaddeus.

"You look so good they'd all be sick with envy," she assured him, and he blushed with pleasure.

The fresh air smelled good as the door slid open. The rain had stopped and a pale sun glared off puddles in the shallows worn in the sidewalk. "Uh-oh," Toby said, seeing the small crowd waiting in the street. A voice called, "Here they are!" and people began to applaud. As if celebrities had come on stage, she thought and, from long exposure to actors, smiled and bowed acknowledgment of the applause.

"What is this?" Thaddeus said, half scared. "What do they want?"

"To meet us," she said through her teeth. "Smile."

"Why? That's weird. We're just two kids."

"And they're twenty adults. Smile."

No one in the crowd was young. Although few looked old, most were like Mr. Milton, past the age of successful rejuvenation. All wore comfortable work suits much like uniforms and a few had on rain capes.

An old man reached out and patted Toby's arm and spoke, but she couldn't understand him. The older the person, the more old-fashioned his language.

"He made your jackets," the woman behind him explained. "He says you look good in them even though he had to use the clothing you came in for a pattern. He says the glue is hardly dry on the seams."

Toby thanked him, and he smiled and was about to speak

again when someone interrupted. "You're not wearing any of the jewelry. You should. We want you to sparkle like the stars you came from." Others murmured agreement.

"What stars?" muttered Thaddeus.

"The jewelry is beautiful," Toby told the audience, "but we can't accept such precious things. Our parents would never allow it."

"How old are you?" called a woman in blue, ignoring Toby's protest.

"Twelve."

"And you were born in a space habitat?"

". . . Yes."

"And you in a starship?"

"Yes, ma'am," Thaddeus said, "The *Alli*—"

"And neither of you has parents here on Earth?"

"No . . ."

The woman wanted to hear no more. "You see," she told the others, "Mr. Milton was right—they did come from the stars. Our prayers are answered."

"What do you mean? We came here because we were hijacked," said Thaddeus. "We were left out there in The Empty, and . . ."

"We'll make you content here," a man interrupted.

"We have animals you can play with," another woman said in tones suitable for enticing reluctant three-year-olds. "Real animals. Not furry robots. Have you ever seen real animals? You'll like them. Habitat children always love animals."

"We'll tell you about our travels. Some of us have led exciting lives."

"You can see the greenhouses. All our food is real. And our flowers."

"And ride horses. You can each have a horse of your own."

"But we won't be here that long," Thaddeus insisted at the first chance of being heard. "We came from the Hillandale Academy and we have to get back to school. Do any of you have a phone, or a radio? Please?"

When no one answered, Toby turned to Orvis. "Would you ask them, please? Maybe they don't understand us."

Orvis repeated Thaddeus's remarks in three different dialects.

Still no one spoke. People looked at the ground, into the distance, anyplace but at the children. In the lull they could hear a hen singing from somewhere behind the house. A hound dog, tail wagging, came trotting down the street, saw Orvis, and decided to go elsewhere.

"Mr. Milton said he'd explained all that to you," the woman in blue said then. She seemed somehow disappointed in them. "We have no contact with the world outside."

"That's what he told us," said Thaddeus. "We didn't believe him."

"It's true," several men said at once.

"Mr. Milton told us that when the aircar was fixed, he'd take us to Lake City," said Toby, "so I don't think you should plan on all those things."

"Fine. We'll go by what the Commander says." The man who had promised them the horses was plainly trying to change the subject. "While you're here, though, let me show you the stables. Better leave the robot behind—I noticed the dog was afraid of him. We wouldn't want to scare the horses."

Toby didn't want to go anyplace with these people but didn't know how to get out of it; she couldn't just run inside and lock the door. A glance at Thaddeus told her he felt the same way, but had no solution either. Still, a walk would give them a chance to see what the place looked like and let them plan how they would escape. "Sure," she said. "Thank you. We'd love to see the horses. Come on, Thaddeus."

Orvis watched them walk away and felt distinctly "left out." Alone again, he sighed, then turned and went the other way, back to the gate they had entered the night before. The people he passed in the streets stepped aside. People working in the greenhouses stared but no one tried to stop him as he crossed the bridge and walked around the walls of the settlement, crossing two more bridges en route.

There were cattle in the field on the north side between the wall and the forest. Their barn formed part of the wall, as did that of the pigs. Orvis listed the doors as two more possible escape routes. Three machinery sheds also opened to the outside. Passing one of the sheds he saw a large robotrac emerge and proceed to a flat grassy oblong, where it lowered gang-plows, cut a swath of sod, and stopped. "Too wet," it said. "Too wet."

"What is your programmed task?" Orvis inquired, puzzled by its actions.

"I am programmed to plant corn. The soil is too wet."

"What else can you do?"

"I am programmed to plant corn. The soil is too wet."

"Yes. Acknowledged," said Orvis. "However—"

"Thank you." With that the robotrac moved away, its tracs throwing clods of mud, several of which struck Orvis on the legs and turret. He sighed again. Conversation with the lower order of machines left much to be desired.

Circling the settlement he climbed a rise, the highest elevation around. From the hilltop he could see the path of the old highway cutting westward through the forest, entering what seemed to be a flat grassland beyond. There was no sign of other human habitation.

Calculating the distance to the horizon and the average walking speed of the two children, he concluded that it would take them approximately three hours to walk as far as he could see. If he sacrificed his principles and allowed them to ride on his back, that time would be cut to thirty minutes. If he carried them all the way to Lake City with no incidents, and good weather, he could make the trip in five hours—six if they had to stop often to drain their waste tanks.

However, upon reaching Lake City he would be seen by any number of people, including officers of the law. Even if the children could protect him from detainment, his freedom would be gone. Once his ID number was fed into the computer, his FARD file would be recalled from the archives and show not only that he had no owner but also that he had disobeyed a court order by leaving the landfill. He could bypass Lake City and take them directly to Fisher's Isle. That would only take another hour. Suppose the great-grandmother person did not want him?

If, on the other hand, he left now, and walked on down that swath of road? Once in the forest, the odds were that he would not be found or so much as seen by humans for months, or ever, if he was careful. He would be free. He would be able to watch birds. He would be alone . . .

Lights blinked all over his body as he free-associated the word *alone*. Solitude was his normal state. Eighty-nine percent of his awareness had been spent in solitude. Why did the thought of being alone now cause this glitch of alarm, as if he were ignoring a command? No one had told him to remain forever with Toby and Thaddeus. They had arbitrarily chosen to divert him from the landfill. They were not responsible for his security, nor he for theirs. Unless he chose to be.

For almost an hour Orvis stood alone on the hill, searching his vast memory, seeking a solution to his unease, some fact that would end this confusion, this sense of *error*, this idea that he was compromising his intellectual integrity. He found thoughts sequenced in Storage, filed under *care* and *feel*. He remembered them as inconclusive, and rapid scanning proved the sequence still illogical—robots could not *care* about humans. Humans could not *care* about robots, except in the sense of mechanical maintenance. That was fact. Yes.

At the end of the hour antennae rose out of his back. He began to transmit an orbiter docking signal. When the signal had been transmitted for fifteen minutes he set off down the hill, heading for the road, for continued freedom, back to being what ORVIS was. The children would be safe until found. And if they weren't found, without his help they would not risk leaving this place of warmth and nourishment. There was no logical reason for him to stay, to lose his freedom, perhaps his existence. He had signaled for pickup and had received two responses: the first a sequential number series, the second an excited voice asking, "Who are you? What are you saying?"

Halfway to the road he looked back. He could see them now, two short, brightly dressed figures followed by nineteen drab adult forms. He walked on, slowly. Toby had set him free, had said robots had souls, had given him lemon oil. Thaddeus treated him as an equal, had asked his opinion on dress. Both had wanted to find a *home* for him. A secure place. This was the object of the trip. They had wanted to do this because they lacked such security for themselves. Now they wanted to leave this place; thus they did not feel secure here.

Orvis sighed.

Their escorted tour took them across the little park. The unkemptness Toby had seen from her window was all around them now. The grass had been ruined by goats, as had most of the plantings. Chickens, geese, and guineas roamed free, using a reflecting pool as a drinking source and swimming hole.

"Why does everything look so messy?" Thaddeus asked undiplomatically.

"We like it that way," said their self-appointed guide. "You spend fifty years in the sterile neatness of a space station and see if you don't yearn for messiness. What you see is our way of rebelling, too, perhaps; a statement about reality."

"Neat is real," said Thaddeus.

"It's also a lot of work," said a man behind them. "Maybe you'd like to help us tidy up?" The adults laughed.

"We were going to put a dome over everything—the base is built—that's the wall—and most of the panels are made and stored in sheds. But now we like being open to the weather. Reality again. Of course, when we get to the age when cold bothers us, we'll have to close it in," their guide went on. "Providing we're still able to by that time."

Toby was only half-listening. She kept thinking of what Orvis had said about heirlooms—wanting to know if he was right, yet concerned that the answer would confirm her worst fears. At last she could bear it no longer. "Are the children who live here away at school?"

"We have no children," said a comparatively young woman in a brown jumpsuit. Several people nodded confirmation. "The few of us who did outlived them—you know how it is. They were gone by the time we got back. But that's why we're so glad you came to visit." Her smile was genuine. "I hope we're not making you nervous by all our attention?"

"A little." Toby tried to return the smile but the knot in her stomach had expanded and now felt like a brick.

"What prayers are we the answer to?" Thaddeus was still trying to get an explanation of that curious statement.

"Oh, that, that was just an expression," the woman said, "meaning that we're glad to see new faces—"

"No!" The word was nearly a shout of protest. As the woman in blue pushed her way to the forefront, the group straggled to an unwilling halt. Toby and Thaddeus moved closer together, sensing trouble.

"You should tell them the truth, Charlotte. Let them know how honored we feel. And why. After all these years." When she turned toward them her eyes were brighter than Mr. Milton's, almost glittering out of her long, bony face. "We *know* there is a Higher Intelligence. But some of us know more. We know the Intelligence that controls both our fates and that of the stars will send us children to take the place of those who have gone back to the stars. We *need* children. When you came, walking out of the night, walking with the robot from the Past, we *knew* you were the first of those children."

"You're wrong." Frightened as she was Toby couldn't let this madness go unchallenged. "You're wrong. We are not those children. You can't keep us here."

"We just found this place by accident," said Thaddeus.

"Nothing is accidental," the woman insisted, "but merely seems so because we can't see the whole vast picture to give it meaning. You were meant to come here."

"Tobyeee . . ." Thaddeus sounded as if he wanted to run.

"That's enough, Andrea." Charlotte put her hand on the other woman's arm and gently pulled her away from the children. "You're frightening them with your wild talk."

"Andrea gets carried away sometimes," the guide said with an easy smile. "We understand her because we're used to her."

Toby looked from his reassuring face back to the woman's bright-eyed-intensity. "But is it true? Do you intend to keep us here?"

"Only until the aircar's fixed. As I said, don't worry about anything. We don't see too many new faces. Some of us forget how to act." He gave Andrea a warning look. "Come on now, let me tell you about our place here. We're rather proud of it. This was all forest when we bought it— all government land. We had it cleared . . ."

For the rest of their tour he kept up a constant commentary which served to inform them as well as to keep his companions from talking too much. Under different circumstances Toby and Thaddeus might have enjoyed themselves, or at least found much of it interesting. They were taken all over the village and shown everything from a distillation plant to the silicon sparger, to a miniature refinery that converted wood into all the necessary hydrocarbons, to a day-old colt, to a nest of kittens so young their eyes had just opened. In the bakery next to the communal kitchen they were introduced to an ancient pastry called doughnuts, which they enjoyed in spite of the situation, and in the dining hall were given an excellent lunch of pot roast with mashed potatoes and gravy.

Their hosts couldn't have been more kind or more attentive. Anything either child said, no matter how flippant or inane, was respectfully listened to, commented on, and repeated for those not close enough to hear the original remark—until Toby began to regret not appreciating these people more. That she felt that way bothered her.

She found herself watching Thaddeus; while she grew more and more nervous he seemed to be more and more at ease, laughing and joking with these old people. She wondered at first if he had gained some courage from their ordeal, until she heard him tell someone, "I used to help the cooks on our ship," and suddenly understood that he felt *at home* here. He had been raised by people like this, a bright little boy among a crew of several hundred adults, more than enough to have made spoiled pets of any children on board. And here he was, being spoiled again by a space-ship crew . . . and liking it.

When Thaddeus asked to see the aircars there was no objection. Everyone walked to a small dome where an almost new, bright yellow, ten-passenger utility van was parked with its power panel removed, the plastic hatch leaning against the outer hull. A service robot stood idle beside the exposed maze of the aircraft's working interior.

"Do you have other aircars?" asked Thaddeus.

"Four. All junkers, but you're welcome to see them."

"No, thank you," said Toby, before Thaddeus could accept. "My feet are sore."

"Excuse us." Thaddeus led her away from the others. "Why did you do that? We might see where they hid the fuel cells."

"No, we wouldn't, or they wouldn't take the chance of showing us," she said. "Don't you see, they think if they flatter and spoil us and give us anything we ask for, we won't want to leave."

He didn't say anything for a while, his gaze on the ground, then still without meeting her eyes, he asked, "Would that be so bad? I mean, I've been thinking; if we stayed here, no one would miss me. They seem to really like us. And there aren't any kids around to pick on me. I could have my own dog, and cats, and a horse. And you wouldn't have to go to Mars. We'd have our own house to live in . . ." He risked a glance up at her then.

Her first impulse was to give way to the panic and anger his suggestion provoked. Yet she knew why he might feel tempted. "If we stayed," she said, "have you thought what we might have to do in return? And would you want to spend the rest of your life in just one place? This place?"

"The ship was only one place. I liked that. And Orvis might be safe here. Think about it."

"We're going to leave here if I have to have Orvis stun you and haul you out like firewood," she told him, frightened.

"I don't really want to stay. Really. Just, sometimes . . . it would be nice . . . Don't be mad at me. You said you were tired of moving. You said, too, you wanted a *permanent* home." His plea for understanding was halted by her sudden and, to Thaddeus, unwarranted laughter.

"What's funny?" he asked, suspecting she was laughing at him.

"Me. I was thinking what it took to make moving to Mars seem like not such a bad idea."

"Children? Would you like some ice cream?"

THIRTEEN

Orvis was waiting by the door when they returned in late afternoon. "Where have you been?" he said. "I was about to initiate a search."

"All over," Thaddeus said wearily.

"We're going to take a nap now," Toby informed the seven people who still followed them. "We'll see you at dinner. Come, Orvis." And without waiting for a response, she hurried in ahead of the robot.

Orvis stopped inside the door. After making sure they were truly alone and both doors were locked, Thaddeus pushed some of the gifts aside before slumping onto the dusty sofa. Toby sprawled on a chair. Both just stared into space, not saying a word.

She'd never been talked to so much in all her life in one day, she thought. These old spacers were worse for talking than actors, although she had to admit they talked less about themselves. Minutes passed in restful silence, the only sound in the room the soft hum of the house fans. Recovering, she sat up to pull off her boots and her glance fastened on Orvis. There was something different about him. "Why are those pink lights flashing on your side? And those two stubby antennae—I never noticed those."

"I am preparing a new map of this settlement and the surrounding area," said Orvis—which she assumed answered her question. "Do you still intend to leave this shelter?"

"This isn't a shelter; it's a trap," she said. "We're going, but we have to wait until everyone is asleep."

"What if Orvis scares the animals and they make noise?" said Thaddeus.

"They will make no noise," said Orvis.

"What if they have a guard watching us all the time?"

"I will stun the guard."

"What if we can't walk all the way?" Thaddeus continued his worrying. "My feet were sore from yesterday and we walked all afternoon in new boots."

"I will carry you on my back," said Orvis, resigned to the compromise of his self-image.

"You mean it?" Thaddeus sat up. "Really?"

"Robots do not lie."

"Thanks! We can take lots of food, and blankets, and—"

"I am a robot, not a truck."

Toby looked at Orvis and was sorry he didn't have a face, or any way to reveal what he thought. He was more human than most humans she knew.

At three in the morning the rear door of the house opened and Orvis stepped out. All his lights were off. After scanning the alley he moved forward. Toby and Thaddeus followed. Both wore two jackets and two pairs of pants against the cool April night. Wrapped in napkins and tucked inside their jackets were apples and sandwiches. At dinner the evening before they'd said how hungry they got at night and their doting audience had vied with one another to prepare snacks.

Orvis was on total alert, all sensors fully activated, as if searching once again for alien life forms. Toby held Thaddeus's hand to keep from being separated in the dark and kept her eye on a shiny spot on Orvis's rear.

The village lay in darkness, the stars the only light. As they had the night before, the choir sang, their voices competing with the far older spring chorus of frogs. High overhead a transcontinental liner passed, tiny points of green and red lights winking.

It seemed to Toby that she had walked for an hour in the less than fifteen minutes it took to reach the barns. She knew where they were more by the odor than by actually being able to see the buildings in the dark. She opened the smaller of the two doors into the cow barn.

Orvis peered inside. "No humans. No sensors. No dogs. Proceed. I will meet you at the outer door." When the door had shut behind them, he hurried around the barns and scaled the wall, an act especially awkward when using only his four good legs.

In the almost total darkness of the barn their best guide

was the squares of dark blue night sky framed by the windows. The cattle were chewing sounds and patches only a little lighter than their surroundings.

"What if we trip over something?" Thaddeus whispered.

"We get up again." she whispered back. "Remember what it looked like this afternoon, in daylight. Head for the middle window, turn left to the door."

Their whispers disturbed a cow, who heaved herself to her feet, tail swishing, hooves clicking on the clean cement. Other cows stirred. Please don't let them moo, Toby silently prayed. When they reached the opposite door neither of them could find the trip mechanism and they nearly panicked until she found it by accident. In the tense dark, both had forgotten that everything in the village was built for adults, placed much higher than things at the Academy.

"You are three minutes late," Orvis said as the door opened. "Follow me." They crossed the paved barnyard apron and tiptoed over the bars of the cattle gate across the creek. On solid ground again, Orvis lowered himself so that they could mount.

There were only two places to sit: one just behind his turret, the other between his midsection and tail. His back was too wide to straddle; they sat with legs folded, Thaddeus in front like a small mahout, Toby behind. Orvis hoisted his dish antenna for Toby to hold onto, or at least that was the reason she assumed.

Riding on a robot was an odd sensation but one she quickly decided she liked. Orvis's back was warm, as if deep-heated from within. She half expected to be motion sick, but even with his limp, his gait was smoother than that of a horse. The only real problems were how to keep from sliding off on the hills, and the soon-to-be painful hardness of the seat. But now, starting out, she clung on and looked back at the village, watching the outline of its rooftops, the color of pale snow, recede behind the trees, hearing the singing fade in the distance.

Orvis followed the ruined highway, his bent leg protesting from the added weight, picking his way through vines and brush and between trees, almost loping when he came to the occasional stretch of intact pavement. He was a tireless mount and an uncomplaining one. By dawn they were twenty miles away. When the sun rose Toby had to ask him to stop so she could stretch her cramped legs and rest her bottom. Both she and Thaddeus had to empty their waste tanks.

Wet weeds brushed against her legs as she made her way down the embankment into the woods. She'd never realized trees could grow as large as those lining this section of the roadbed. The trees around the Academy were big compared to those in the habitats, but these dwarfed any in her experience. She tried to measure the oak she'd chosen for privacy and discovered that, with arms outstretched, it would take four and one-half people her size to reach around the trunk. The thought that a plant could be so massive, so old, and so sure of its place in the world awed her. On impulse she pressed herself against the giant and hugged the rough gray trunk.

She was almost back to the road when Orvis warned,

"An aircraft is approaching from the southeast."

"They found us! I knew they'd find us!" Thaddeus ran toward a wide strip of roadway ahead, waving his arms to make sure he was seen, shouting wildly. "Here we are! Over here! Over here!"

"Come back!" she called. "Thaddeus! What if it's the spacers?" But he was making too much noise to hear.

She saw the dish antenna on Orvis's back rapidly rotate and tip. When she looked in the direction its center rod pointed, she saw a yellow van come into view, the same van they'd seen in the village hangar.

"Thaddeus!" Her cry was almost a scream. "Hide! Hide, Orvis!" She ran for the shelter of the tall trees. Halfway there she looked back; Thaddeus was just standing there, staring up at the airvan in shock as it descended. She slowed and stopped, hesitated, and then went back to get him, her boots slipping on the rolling leaves covering the slope. "Come on!" She grabbed him by the arm and pulled him after her.

Orvis waited where he stood, the light on his rear rod antenna flashing, the dish slowly rotating. One camera eye watched the children run down the slope and dodge behind a tree; one monitored and identified the yellow craft landing on the pavement ahead; two scanned the sky, searching for visual verification of the transmission he was receiving from a second aircraft approaching from the northwest.

"Lake City Control? This is three-eight-five again. That signal the liner reported? We're still receiving. No. No identification. The pilot thought it was a fallen satellite but we can't confirm. Besides, the thing keeps moving—or did until the last few minutes. No report of downed satellites? Okay. The same one reported yesterday. Yeah. It's an automatic distress call of some sort. We can't get a vocal response. Hold on! There's a message on our screen . . . It says: 'Toby West and Thaddeus Hall are in danger. Continue on present landing coordinates. Beware yellow craft bearing Serial Number 847347OH. Please acknowledge receipt of message and assist.' "

"We read you. Please identify yourself," the patrol car ordered.

"I am ORVIS."

There was muffled speech from the patrol car and then, "Who are you, Orvis? And where are you?"

But the robot had said all that was necessary.

"Toby? Thaddeus?" Their names echoed among the trees and a squirrel began to scold. "You can't escape. If you try, you'll get lost again. You'll die of exposure and starvation." Mr. Milton stood beside the yellow van and waited for a response. When none came he said, "Why can't you accept us? We'll be good to you. The stars sent you to us, to help us as we age, to take our places. Your coming to us was no accident. The stars dictated your path."

"I wish the stars would send him home," Thaddeus muttered.

"Shhh." She was trying to hear a distant sound—as if a second aircar were coming.

"Your robot is running away!" Mr. Milton sounded so

pleased that Thaddeus would have stepped out to see for himself if Toby hadn't stopped him.

"He's lying. Don't listen."

"You sure?"

"Orvis wouldn't leave us. Not now."

"Do you want us to hunt you down?" Mr. Milton called. "We can."

The word *hunt* reminded Toby of a film Lillian had made about ancient Earth when dogs were used to find runaway people. *Bloodhounds of Alabama*, that was the title. Maybe this second aircar was bringing the dogs? She remembered seeing two dogs in the village that resembled the hounds used in the picture. Except the film dogs were all robots; real dogs were too expensive and hard to train.

"You go down that way. You people circle out." Mr. Milton was shouting directions. "Forget the robot; get the children. They have to be here. We'd have heard them running in the leaves otherwise." Then he added, apparently in answer to a question, "Yes, if you have to, stun them. We're too old to run them down."

This is real, Toby reminded herself as she pressed her back against the tree and heard her heart thumping in her ears. Thaddeus and I are here, it's morning, on the surface of Earth, and we are going to be hunted down and captured by crazy people. Our only hope of rescue is an antique robot. Why should reality feel so unreal?

Dead branches crackled beneath the feet of their hunters. Thaddeus gave a little hiss of fear and squeezed her hand so hard it hurt. Just then one of the villagers stepped from behind a tree not thirty feet away. It was Andrea, the woman in blue.

"Look!" Thaddeus breathed in her ear. "Want to run for it?"

"No," she said after thinking it over. "Let's go back to where Orvis is. He'll protect us."

"You're sure he's there?"

"Yes!"

They were climbing over the high buttressing roots of the big tree when Toby stepped on a dead branch and snapped it. "Here!" the woman yelled. She stood on the slope above, pointing a stungun at them. "Here they are!"

Toby raised her arms in surrender, the way prisoners always did in films, and began to climb the embankment back to the road. She'd never realized how much raising one's arms affected balance and slowed a person down, especially on hills. She turned to see if Thaddeus was with her. He was, hands clasped behind his neck, head tilted up to see the sky.

"Toby, look!" he yelled suddenly. "Over there. Look at the flashing lights! A patrol car's coming!" As he spoke the sound of the aircraft reached them clearly, the forest seeming to echo and magnify the wail of the siren.

"Come to me!" Mr. Milton ordered, looking from them to the air patrol car. "Don't try to run to them. We're going to convince these officers that we are on an outing. You're going to help us. You'll agree with whatever we say. Do you understand? I will not spend the last few years of my life in some miserable rehab clinic."

Why is Orvis letting him do this? Toby thought. Why doesn't he stun them all?

"Where's Orvis?" Thaddeus pivoted on a heel. "Where is he, Toby? You said he'd be here."

"We'll see him in a minute, as soon as we get to the top of the hill." But the top of the slope, the roadbed, Mr. Milton and the villagers, all were already in plain view and Orvis was not. She stopped so quickly that Thaddeus bumped into her. "He did run away . . ." She couldn't believe it. They were on their own and that sudden understanding stunned her.

"Into the van," Mr. Milton ordered, running toward them as the patrol car landed. "Now!" When he grabbed Toby by the arm she could feel each of his fingers through the sleeves of her jackets. His grip was as real as the sour smell of his breath.

"No!" She tried to jerk away. When he didn't let her go, she kicked his left shin as hard as she could.

"My varicosity!" He let her go to clutch his leg, hobbling on one foot.

"Run, Thaddeus!" She headed toward the patrol car, her feet slipping on the wet leaves.

She'd never been shot and didn't know anyone who had, but as she ran she was expecting to be hit in the back. In films the actor shot always jumped at the impact of the fake charge, or yelled, or grimaced and clutched his middle—which suggested that getting shot by a stungun caused severe pain. But all the actors she'd ever asked didn't know if that was true. "Who cares?" one had said. "It's only entertainment." She found that being threatened by the real thing lacked entertainment value.

Preoccupied, she failed to look where she was going and ran directly across the space the patrol car had chosen to land. The whoosh of air as the pilot abruptly veered and lifted startled her; she yelled, ducked, and tripped over a stone. The ground came up to meet her and she *oofed* with the impact.

"Toby!" Thaddeus caught up to her, yanking her to her feet. "Get up! They're going to catch us!"

"Drop those weapons!" The speaker on the patrol car was so loud it hurt her ears. "Everyone freeze!" As she raised her head the white and green aircar filled her view, setting down only yards away. Before it touched ground a door slid open; an officer natty as an insect in black boots, black pants, and a brown jacket jumped out.

"Toby West? Thaddeus Hall?"

"Yes, sir," said Thaddeus. "We—"

"Get in the car. Move! I'll get her."

"We were merely trying to rescue them," Mr. Milton said, still massaging his shin. "When they saw us land, they panicked. I'm told lost children frequently do that . . ."

She was starting to get up when the officer grabbed her by the waist and carried her to the car as if she were a rag doll. As he deposited her on the rear seat she saw his pilot partner, gun drawn, standing beside the car. "You hurt?" Her rescuer's eyes were hidden by the sun visor of his white helmet.

"No, sir." Her knees hurt and she was still bruised from

the day the men kidnapped Sanders, but she suspected this was no time to go into details.

"Good. Stay there. Help coming?" This question was directed to the pilot as their rescuer slid the door half-shut.

"Two cars and the medvan," said the pilot. "Where's the guy with the weird transmitter? What's-his-name?"

"Orvis." The officer turned and leaned around the door. "Where's Orvis? What sort of vehicle is he driving?"

"What?" Thaddeus was genuinely confused by the question.

"Who's Orvis?" said Toby.

Fifty yards upslope, from the hollow of an uprooted tree, Orvis's sensor array monitored the scene, although part of his view was obscured by the hairy root tangles that camouflaged him. Standing in a pool of water with leaves and muck below, he saw the air patrol car land and the children bundled into it and safety.

He watched the other two police cars arrive, and the medvan, which came in shrieking of its own importance and to which the children were promptly escorted. Once they were inside this craft he monitored the transmission of their vital signs—all acceptable—to an orbiting satellite and simultaneously watched the village people being collected into a motley group for questioning. When Toby and Thaddeus were returned from the medvan to the patrol car and that car lifted off, Orvis watched it go. The medvan left next, siren off. He stayed to see the villagers board the two remaining patrol cars and their van flown away by a uniformed officer.

Another patrol car arrived then, sensors protruding from its body. Instead of landing, it cruised overhead in a slow circle. Analyzing the situation, Orvis concluded that the purpose of this craft was to locate himself, the transmitter of the pickup signal. He instantly shut down all systems for a period of two hours and became, for all measurable purposes, a discarded hulk.

When his timer turned him on again he found himself alone, the mid-morning sun obscured by clouds. In that time gravity on his inert mass had pushed him almost knee-deep into the muck below. A rock weighing 3.2 pounds had slid down from the root mass onto his right front foot, and an enterprising squirrel, finding the robot's back warmer than the surrounding terrain, had begun to build a leafy nest beneath his dish antenna.

Orvis sighed and patiently began to free himself. At his first movement the squirrel leaped to the safety of an over-hanging hazel bush and clung there swaying, as if to make sure of the need to abandon such a cozy nesting site. After a brief struggle, Orvis stood on the bank, black mud and rotting vegetation still clinging to his legs. The squirrel had long since fled.

A robin caught his attention. Poised beneath a silver ma-ple, its head cocked to one side, the bird was obviously listening for prey moving beneath the surface. Orvis stopped to watch and appreciate the bird's excellent hearing and his own solitude. There was no human now to scare wild life forms, or to be frightened by them.

After considering the implications of that thought for thirty-two seconds, Orvis sighed. The robin flew away.

FOURTEEN

From the control panel a dispatcher's clipped voice murmured of lawbreakers, emergencies, and locations. The patrol car interior smelled of boot polish, old plastic, and muddy clothing.

"How did you know they wouldn't shoot us?" Thaddeus asked. They were looking out the windows at the buildings down below, the outlying factories and greenhouse domes of Lake City. To the north, Lake Erie blended with the sky like a vast inland sea.

"I didn't," said Toby. "I expected to be shot."

He didn't answer for a long time and then took a deep breath before saying, "It's a good thing I trust you. If I had known you thought that I never would have run after you." He leaned forward and tapped the male officer on the shoulder. "Where are we going?"

"Mrs. Philips's place."

"We'll be landing in about two minutes." The pilot turned in her seat to give them a reassuring smile. "Your grandmother is waiting for you."

"My great-grandmother," Toby said automatically, struck by the idea that less than fifteen minutes' flying time had been between them and safety, and between the villagers and the world they had closed out.

"Whatever," said the pilot. "Now, in case there's a crowd and lots of lights and reporters when we set down, don't be alarmed. Just stick close to us."

"How would reporters know you found us?" Toby couldn't remember hearing either officer talk to anyone but the dispatcher.

"Reporters monitor the emergency channels," came the pilot's bored reply.

"You wouldn't have any way of knowing," the male officer explained, "but you've been a hot news item ever since you turned up missing. Two rich ex-Terran kids, lost in The Empty. People *love* that stuff. Especially the ones up in the glass bubbles. Lots of people were out hunting for you. They just didn't know where to look. Your pilot was way off course when he picked those two boonies up. His nav-system was totally screwed up, I hear. And he didn't even know it. The old guy hadn't flown more than twenty miles from home in years."

"Did you find Mr. Sanders? Did those men . . . ?" Thaddeus couldn't bring himself to voice his fear.

"The chauffeur's fine," the pilot said. "Or he will be when he gets out of the medcenter. He was left unconscious in the truck when the Johnson brothers dumped it to steal a faster car."

"The Johnson brothers!" Thaddeus pounced on the name. "That's who the space people said it was. They said the Johnson brothers stole their pigs."

"Figures," said the patrolman.

"Most people who live in The Empty have psychological problems," the pilot said. "Some who go out there are sociopaths—they can't stand being with people. Some are druggies. Some are natives, inbred, simple-minded—like the group called the Johnson Family. They're actually a gang, not necessarily related. The law tries to keep track of troublemakers, but in such a big area . . ."

"Yeah." The man took over the conversation again. "These two guys were born out there. Talk about needing birth quotas. Typical boonie trash. Always in trouble. Always giving us grief. In the past ten years they've been in eleven State psych-rehab centers between them—a real waste of taxpayers' credits. You can't rehab people who were nothing but trouble to start with." He frowned with disapproval at such pampering of criminals. "I miss the good old days when the State vaporized . . ." He glanced beneath his lids at the rear seat and decided not to finish the thought aloud. "They are not nice men," he concluded, belatedly aware of his audience.

"They took our sandwiches." Thaddeus's tone suggested there were some acts too mean ever to be forgiven. "Did you catch them yet?"

"We will. Don't worry about it."

"What will happen to them?"

"They'll get free room and board."

"What will happen to the people from the village?"

"It depends on what they end up accused of doing to you."

"We wanted to use the phone and they wanted to keep us," Thaddeus summarized. "But, except when we tried to escape, they were nice. They're lonesome I think. They just want to have some children. And it would be a good place for children whose parents are out in space," he added thoughtfully. "They understand—"

"That's Fisher's Isle there, below and to your left," the pilot interrupted.

Wind gusts buffeted the car as Toby looked down. The only thing she could see below was water, green and choppy. As the car began to bank into a landing approach she suddenly felt uneasy; being aware of this volume of liquid made her feel as vulnerable as being in deep space.

Then land came into view, reassuring bluffs along the lake shore, surmounted by trees and groupings of faceted domes covering what looked like endless acres of green vegetable crops. Other domes looked pink and white from the flowering trees inside. Rows of maples flanked an open meadow separating the greenhouse domes from a large building on the highest bluff and extended around the bluff for some distance. Although the house plainly had been built to withstand the winter winds off the lake—the walls were curved and angled, the roofs planed like airfoils—the entire structure was covered by a dome of its own. Was *this* where Goldie lived?

Computer spoke with computer and the pilot surrendered control to the autopilot, saying, "We'll be landing in the private hangar, not their freight depot." As they banked around the large building dome an open hangar came into view, its platform crowded with aircraft and people.

"How's that for a house, Sergeant?" the pilot asked her partner, who responded with an admiring whistle.

"It must be bigger than the Learning Center!" said Thaddeus. "What does she do with so much space?"

Toby shook her head, not wanting to admit she was as surprised as he was to see the place. When she'd called, the vuphone picture had given no hint of this. But a phone wouldn't, she thought, since it used a close-up lens. She had assumed again, because Lillian had referred to her as "Poor Mother, living in that awful place." Looking down on the real property, it was obvious that when Lillian said "Poor Mother," she wasn't referring to the old lady's financial status.

As the aircar put down in the hangar, the hiss of its jets grew louder and mingled with the rumble of the closing dome. Catching a glimpse of the overhead dome sliding shut, Toby felt a twinge of anxiety, as if she were being closed away from Earth again, shut into a future she never would have chosen. The aircar shuddered as it touched the floor. Some thirty people—not one of whom looked familiar—stood in a ragged half-circle, waiting. Film lights were on; more were being set up. Behind the lights was a white airvan with a blue logo and the word NAVideo on its side. Next to it was another patrol car with warning lights flashing, sending blurs of brilliant green and white over the area. Two black rental limos and a service truck were parked in front of a row of aircraft that appeared to belong in the hangar.

As she sat forward to see if there was anyone she knew outside, lights flashed into her eyes and she realized she was being filmed through the glass. Blinking, she sank back against the seat, trying to get out of sight. The persistent cameraman pressed his lens against the pane.

The officers got out first and pushed the cameramen back, ignoring the shouted questions. As if the person who yelled the loudest would get answered first, Toby thought. From the flashing patrol car two more officers emerged and tried, without much success, to control the crowd.

"When they said 'reporters' I didn't know what they meant." Thaddeus twisted nervously on the back seat, trying to see out of all the windows at once. "This is scarier than everything else."

"It'll be okay," Toby said vaguely. She was trying to see where Goldie was.

"Behave yourselves!" one of the patrolmen yelled. "The Philipses gave permission for you people to land in here at our request, to avoid possible midair accidents. You all promised to abide—"

"Where are the kids?" a man called.

"Let us talk to them!" another shouted.

"Let's be civilized," the pilot pleaded. "They've been through a lot."

As the pilot spoke, a man slid open the car door and held out his hand to Toby. "Miss West, could you step out here, please? You, too, little boy. I'm sure the family's on the way over from the house. In the meantime, perhaps you'd both be kind enough to answer our questions?"

"You can't do that!" The pilot and patrolman started to intervene, then hesitated, intimidated by the sight of all the cameras on them.

This isn't real, Toby thought as she slid off the seat and stepped onto the concrete, reluctant to make a scene. She was holding onto Thaddeus with one hand and trying to shield her eyes from the lights with the other. The lakefront air in the hangar was cold and she shivered in her damp clothing. A black stick suddenly poked at her teeth, bending against her cheek. She flinched away before seeing it was only a microphone.

"Can you tell us how it feels to be here? Were you ill-treated by the hijackers?" A hand plucked at her shoulder and she jerked away.

"Hey, Thaddeus? What can you tell us?"

"Where did you get that name, son?"

"I hate interviewing kids," Toby heard a woman whisper. "It's like talking to a stone."

Through a gap between reporters and policemen Toby saw, on the opposite side of the hangar, a large, white-haired woman in a bulky gray sweater. She was getting out of what appeared to be a conveyor cab from a lower level, looking at the crowd with a bemused expression.

"Goldie!" She dodged between bodies, pushing them aside, tugging Thaddeus along. "Goldie!" she called again. The woman saw her and broke into a smile, then simply opened her arms and waited in welcome.

Hugging Goldie reminded Toby of hugging the old tree, and not only because she couldn't begin to reach around. Like the tree, the woman was sturdy and sure of her place on the earth; better yet, she felt warm and soft and smelled of good perfume. And no tree could ruffle your hair with a soft dry hand and let you know how glad it was to see you.

"I don't see my huge present." Goldie leaned away to look at them, her blue eyes bright with tears of welcome. "They found Sanders and the truck, but you two and my present were still missing. Now you're here but still no gift."

"He had to hide when the patrol car came," Thaddeus said in a whisper.

"Oh?" Goldie looked to Toby for an explanation. "What were you bringing me?"

"A robot—"

"An antique robot," Thaddeus interrupted. "He's been to—"

"You'd have liked Orvis," Toby went on. "He saved our lives." She had to turn away to blink back tears, much to her disgust. She couldn't imagine what was wrong; she wasn't normally a crybaby.

"Chin up!" Goldie's voice dropped to a conspiratorial

whisper and she gave their arms an affectionate little squeeze. "We'll talk later. Right now it's Show Time."

"Don't mention Orvis," Toby whispered.

"Right." Goldie nodded and straightened up to face the approaching reporters.

"Are you pressing criminal charges against the spacer cult?" a woman asked. "Do you think they're insane?" She smiled encouragingly, to indicate her empathy if they said yes.

"I don't know what that means, but they're not criminals," said Thaddeus.

"Just because they live in The Empty doesn't mean they're crazy." To her surprise Toby found herself defending them. "How would you like to feel you didn't belong on your own planet? And nobody here cared?"

"Lots of people coming back from space feel that way," Thaddeus added. "Nobody helped them either. They hated the reorientation center."

"Then try a mental health clinic," the woman quipped and was met by laughter.

"Tabitha," a man called with unwarranted familiarity in his voice. "I saw the medical report when you were picked up by the air patrol. Were the spacers the ones who hurt you? Did they make you do anything you didn't want to?"

"No!" said Toby, angry. "That was the hijackers . . ."

That was when Goldie intervened, placing her arms around Toby and Thaddeus. "Thank you, ladies and gentlemen. The children are tired. I know you don't want to add to their ordeal. My staff will see you out of my hangar."

That was the picture used on the news that night: Goldie with her arms encircling their shoulders, Toby and Thaddeus cuddling against her as if she were their maternal refuge. For viewers conditioned to the slick artifice of their time there was a crude honesty to both the woman's appearance and the children's vulnerable pose that shocked as well as moved. In weeks to come sociologists would label the still photo made of that shot "the most disturbing picture of the decade." Some would credit it with changing styles, and the faddish return to natural aging. Lillian would term the shot "tacky, but with raw dramatic impact."

"Are my parents coming?" Toby asked when they were safely in the conveyor cab, gliding through the tunnel connecting the main house and the hangar.

"Yes. Lillian, too. Of course, they won't get here much before next Monday . . ." For the first time Goldie looked uncomfortable. "I'm afraid they somehow got the initial impression you'd run away to avoid transferring to a school on Mars—and that I was somehow involved."

"Why would they think that?"

"Lillian. Your parents were on location so Dr. Ebert called her. As soon as she heard you were on your way here she lost her temper and wouldn't listen."

"She assumed," said Toby, anger creeping into her voice. "Orvis is right; assuming is a mistake."

"The robot." Goldie brightened at the mention of him.

"Tell me—No. We won't have time now. We'll talk in your rooms."

The cab slid up a mild incline into a lobby where sunlight made velvety carpets glowing islands of red on the polished marble floor. Waiting there were at least fifty people, and more could be seen hurrying in through the archway at the back of the lobby.

"More reporters?" Toby said before seeing that half the group were children and several of the adults looked rather like her mother.

"Employees and their families, and your great-uncles and aunts and cousins. They didn't want to come out to the hangar and add to the commotion."

Seeing names on a genealogy chart was one thing; seeing the people those names represented was another. A pleased and rather foolish grin lighted Toby's face. She had a *family*, a real family.

"Do they all *live* here?" said Thaddeus.

"Yes, but you can learn names later. They just want to say hello and then they promised to let you go so you can have some lunch and get settled."

"No wonder the place is so big. Look, Toby!" He pointed to a banner held by three children. WELCOME HOME TOBY AND THADDEUS had been hurriedly painted in bold but messy red letters.

"You're family now, too, Thaddeus." The car came to a gentle stop and Goldie pushed herself to her feet. "After Dr. Ebert told us why your parents couldn't be notified, we all took a vote and decided to adopt you. Now you'll al-

ways have a place here on Earth to call home. Like Toby.
Is that all right with you?"

Thaddeus looked up at her and nodded enthusiastic
agreement, too pleased to talk, then punched Toby's arm,
and the two children grinned at each other.

As the cab door slid open they were greeted with a cheer
and applause. Two tiny children clutching bouquets of
roses were pushed forward to present the flowers in greeting.

Until you actually saw them, and got to know them,
things and people were never as you imagined them to be,
thought Toby, as she allowed herself to be hugged and
kissed and introduced. That was probably because your
imagination was based on your private point of view and
plain ignorance. And in the case of Goldie, prejudiced impressions from Lillian and her mother. She'd always imagined Goldie, when thinking of her at all, as living by her
lonesome, with perhaps a few faithful employees like Sanders, in a place that resembled the Academy's barns, but
older and shabbier. The extent of her ignorance made her
blush.

Looking around, she saw Thaddeus being kissed by a
girl cousin and patted on the back by several boys. It was
the first time she'd ever seen him look truly happy; acceptance made his whole face come alive. He even looked
taller to her. As if feeling her gaze he turned and with a
smile just for her alone mouthed. "Thank you," and she
wanted very much to hug him.

Lillian would see he had star quality, she thought. If she

doesn't . . . when I grow up I'll find the right script for him and prove it. Unless he outgrows it . . . some child stars do—at ten they're charming and at fifteen they turn into pumpkins. But Thaddeus won't lose it, unless he gets too happy.

And then she stopped, appalled. She had been *casting*, just as her parents did, as Lillian did, when they met people. And it was fun! And then she realized that she had automatically assumed that making films would be part of her future.

Perhaps it wasn't so bad a thing to do . . .

But she wouldn't make stupid fantasies. Real things were more interesting. Think of the story she could do on the spacers! Or Orvis. And films about Earth. Especially about The Empty. She could show habitat people how nice Earth was, and how much they'd given up—all the room, and the sky, and air. Instead of alien monsters or love-in-a-habitat, she could excite people with reality.

Maybe the school on Mars would be a good idea. But surely there were schools on Earth that taught the same thing. She could major in media in college and then when she graduated—

"Toby? Are you all right, dear? You seem a million miles away." Goldie was beside her, smiling, but concerned. "You must be so tired, both of you. Come, let's collect Thaddeus and I'll walk you down to the guest wing."

Their rooms were large and lush. The beds were antiques; there were delicate chairs, and the carpets were thick and velvety. Thaddeus's room overlooked Lake Erie and the bathroom had a fireplace—for which Toby envied him. But her windows overlooked an inner courtyard where espaliered peach trees bloomed in the afternoon sun, and that view pleased her even more.

"Now. At last." Goldie sighed with relief as she settled into a comfortable chair in Toby's room. "Sit down, please. Lunch will be coming soon. While we wait you can start to tell me about this robot. Orvis."

Telling about Orvis took a long time, for they had to recount almost all of their adventure. Lunch came, was eaten, and the plates removed before the story was finished. Goldie, being a good listener, asked only the questions needed to understand or help the tale along. She was satisfyingly indignant on the subject of their hijackers, calling them "wicked" and promising to do all she could to see that they were punished.

"Mr. Milton and his people seem more desperate than wicked," she decided when she heard about the villagers' gifts and their general kindness. "Do you think they should be punished?"

"No," said Toby. "I feel sorry for them—now that I'm safely here."

"I liked them," said Thaddeus. "Especially the ones I could understand. Even a couple I couldn't."

"I don't know what the legal outcome of all this will be, but if the space people will allow it, I'm going to try to help them," said Goldie.

"They'd make good foster grandparents for kids like

me," said Thaddeus. "They really understand what time in space does to people . . . and families."

"That's a very good idea." Goldie nodded thoughtfully. "And perhaps not only for children whose parents are in space." Thaddeus beamed with her approval.

"I'm sorry Orvis ran away," Goldie said when their story was finished, "although I would have in the same situation. I am especially sorry because, if you hadn't met him, you wouldn't have come to see me. So in several ways Orvis is responsible for giving me a great deal of pleasure. He would have been welcome here, and I would have enjoyed his company. He could sort and recatalogue the books in the library, if he wanted to keep busy. I've been meaning to have someone get at that . . ." She stared out the window and her words trailed off into a sigh.

At that Toby and Thaddeus exchanged a look and smiled at their shared memory, and then Thaddeus was overcome by a yawn so wide his eyes teared and his jawbone creaked. Before she could control it, Toby yawned in sympathy.

After Thaddeus excused himself and went off to bed, Goldie made sure the door was closed before asking Toby, "How much don't you want to transfer to the school on Mars?"

"A lot!"

"I should keep out of this, but . . . I can make Lillian change her mind."

"How?" said Toby, excited by the thought of being able to return to the Academy with Thaddeus, of spending holidays together here, of really getting to know her Terran cousins, and most of all, being able to stay on Earth.

"I'm a major stockholder in Infield Productions."

Toby frowned. "I thought the company was all Lillian's. She always calls it *my* company."

Goldie smiled. "Trust me. I can convince my daughter that sending you off to Mars is not a wise idea."

"You'd do to her what she does to my parents? Control her with money?"

"It works," Goldie said simply.

"I don't think I like the idea." Toby was going to add, "I don't want you to come down to her level," but didn't.

"But you don't seem to believe you have any chance of defying her," Goldie prompted when Toby fell silent. "Or your parents."

"Not if they don't back me up," admitted Toby. "My parents always do whatever she says. And in a way that's nice for them. So long as they let her make all the decisions they don't have any more real responsibility than I do. They don't have to grow up . . ." She paused, distracted by this bit of insight into her parents' characters, and her own.

"When I grow up, I'll make sure Lillian has no control over *me*."

Goldie smiled to herself, as if this resolve confirmed something she had suspected. "You're rather like her, you know. No. Don't get more angry. Listen. Lillian may just understand if you tell her how you feel. She's quite independent herself. She never forgave her father and me for bringing her back to Earth. We were so homesick . . . She was born in the Greenhouse. That was 'home' to her. She wanted nothing to do with Earth—had nothing but contempt for what she called the 'Old World.' What made it worse was that we wanted more children—which of course we couldn't have there, with the quotas and all. She was a habitat child—and she was humiliated to be the daughter of such old-fashioned parents. When her brothers were born she ignored them . . . they didn't exist for her."

Goldie poured herself a cup of coffee before continuing. Toby waited patiently, noticing the cup rattled slightly on its saucer as the old woman lifted it.

"We didn't know how unhappy she was here until she graduated from Hillandale. She wouldn't come home with us. She went straight to the Greenhouse, to college. She's never come back to Earth—that I know of." Goldie's glance rested on Toby's face and moved on. "Not once. Not even when her father died. I was shocked when she said she was coming now. You must mean a lot to her."

Remembering that Lillian *had* come to Earth to visit her daughter, twice, Toby was too polite to say she thought it unlikely that she meant much to Lillian, that any person did. How could you not come to see Goldie? How could you hurt her like that? After a moment she asked, "How old was Lillian when you moved back to Earth?"

"Seven." Goldie somehow looked much older as she remembered the child who had been hers. Then, meeting Toby's thoughtful eyes, she reached out and enclosed the girl's hand in her own, plump and freckled, and gently squeezed. "All things pass, they say. If you live long enough." Her ruby ring winked red in the light as she rather stiffly rose to her feet. "You must want to bathe and get some sleep. I must see to my lettuce deliveries. A produce business doesn't stop just because company comes."

"What do you produce?" Toby suddenly realized she didn't know.

Goldie frowned, as if it were an odd question. "Why . . . Philips is the largest fruit and vegetable farm in the country. We ship worldwide and off-world. That's how the Greenhouse got its name. We designed the gardens and supplied the plantings. We were going to expand from there . . . Lillian never told you this?"

Toby shook her head.

"Strange." Goldie puzzled a bit, then dismissed everything with a shrug. "That's her loss. You'd better get some rest."

Toby watched her leave the room, noticing for the first time that her great-grandmother limped slightly as she walked. Like Orvis, she was old. Somehow thinking of the two of them made her start to cry. She thought she was crying for grief at losing the robot, and while that was partially true, some of her tears came from the unconscious knowledge that she was growing up, some from knowing that time would cause her to lose Goldie, too—and some from complete physical exhaustion. Five minutes later she was fast asleep.

FIFTEEN

Orvis walked overland, where the trees grew thickest, threading his way among wooded hills that marked the buried ruins of a city, splashing through creeks and bogs, twice crossing small lakes by walking across the bottom. The tracks he left behind in mud suggested the footprints of a very large, very odd bird. Anyone observing his direct northwest path would have assumed he had a goal, a destination, but he was aware of none. As he walked he talked to himself, aloud, which was most unlike him.

"I am a multi-purpose unit, self-contained, self-repairing— within reason—and self-assured," he said at one point, and then as his right front foot struck a rock and metal sang, he added, "Also self-absorbed. For the past five miles I remember nothing I have seen."

He stopped, disturbed by that. To move on automatic could result in damage or destruction. Where had he set himself to go, and why? He immediately ran a systems check and, upon remembering his original destination, monitored his present surroundings. He reminded himself of his solitary state. Why was he using his speakers?

There was no evidence of living humans. The air smelled of forest floor, much like the mulch his second owner had spread around tubbed bushes. To the left a colony of—he searched his botanical data for an identification and found—*skunk cabbage* was pushing up leaves along a creek. Beside him was a ... *dogwood* tree, leaf and flower buds thickening with new growth. In the stillness he could hear hundreds of insects, including eleven separate varieties of beetle larvae encased and chewing inside the fallen tree to his right. Frogs, toads, and birds were singing. Then from high overhead came the voices of wild geese. Currents stirred within his mind. His turret moved as he brought into focus three dark skeins of geese against the night sky. Also headed north.

"Birds of passage," he said, watching. "Sojourners. Like myself. Yet they are in the company of their kind while I am a solitary unit with no company of any kind. They fly with purpose. I am a multi-purpose unit ... but I have no purpose. With no purpose I am nothing but metal and memory."

Toby slept the clock around and woke at 2:00 A.M. happily surprised to see and remember where she was. She'd been dreaming the three of them were walking endlessly around the wall of the village, lost and cold. Now she saw that the walls of her room glowed a sunrise pink except for the window wall, where fabric shut out the night.

Her mind drifted back to the dream, the villagers, and the men who had taken the truck.

Living in isolation of any kind did odd things to people's minds. Maybe that was why the habitats became so popular—after they quit being a necessity. You were never alone there, unless you chose to be. And from what she'd seen, people liked being alone about as much as sparrows did. It made them think too much, or too differently. As she was doing now. She kicked off the covers and saw she'd fallen asleep before taking a bath or putting on night-clothes.

After bathing and brushing her teeth, she put on her pajamas and then crossed the hall to see if Thaddeus might be up. All his lights were on but he was sleeping, still snoring with exhaustion. A tray of food sat untouched on a table near his bed. She found she was disappointed that he wasn't awake. They hadn't had a chance to talk alone since being in the woods that morning. That seemed so long ago. And when tomorrow came, all sorts of people would be around. It was odd how you could miss a person when he was right beside you.

She sat down carefully on the edge of his bed, noticing how long his lashes were against his cheeks; how, though his arms were flung above his head, he had both fists clenched; how young he looked. He smiled in his sleep and she wondered if he was dreaming of being back home, aboard his ship—if he wanted to go back. She thought he did most of the time. It was odd but she couldn't think of any time or place she wanted to go back to. That made her feel alone.

How had Lillian been able to bear staying away from here all these years? And was she really coming because she cared about her—or was it just an excuse to see Goldie and her home again? If she . . .

Thaddeus abruptly flopped over on his side, perhaps disturbed by her presence. She jumped up and fled back to her room, feeling vaguely guilty at having invaded his privacy. Only then did she notice a covered tray on her table. Someone had come in while she slept and left it, and probably stood watching her sleep.

Turning on the entertainment screen to music and colors, she drank the milk and ate the sandwich of lettuce and thinly sliced chicken. After one bite of cake she fell asleep in the chair. When her lolling head made her neck hurt she managed to waken enough to stagger to her bed and slept soundly until six in the morning.

The angle of morning light made the peach trees blaze with pink. Three robins were bouncing over the lawn, each careful to keep to its own territory. How did they get under the dome? Yellow and purple crocuses bloomed around the peach trees. It was too lovely a day to waste in bed. Putting on the blue sweatsuit and shoes someone had laid out for her, she went out into the garden. The cool air smelled of peach blossoms, grass, and the lake.

From the windows of her room the garden looked enclosed, but as she walked along the crocus bed she saw the lawn stretched around the end of the house and over to a wide driveway which led through an open arch. The air was colder here and when she stepped outside, wind ruffled her hair and made her wish for a sweater. Still, no one else was awake, and to feel a place this big was yours in the quiet of the morning was worth a shiver or two. Besides, the driveway along the maples looked like a great place to run. Exercise would warm her.

Half a mile and she was panting. Coming on a sturdy wooden bench with a view over the lake, she plopped down gratefully and mopped her forehead with her sleeve. She had been sitting there long enough to start shivering again when she imagined she hard a familiar noise.

CRee-ECH . . . CReeECH-clack! CRee-ECH.

She stood up and looked around, up and down the drive-way, between the greenhouse domes across the way. Nothing. Telling herself she was imagining things, she sat down again.

CRee-ECH. CReeECH-clack. CRee-ECH.

It wasn't her imagination. The sound was real and com-ing from the water—or near the water. When the wind dropped she heard it clearly. Getting up, she walked toward the edge of the grassy bluff and scanned the shoreline. Down there, coming along the beach, was Orvis. With all six legs spread wide for traction on the wet stone and gravel slope, he had never looked more awesome, more insectlike. To Toby he was beautiful.

She went down the bluff slipping and sliding, as often on the seat of her pants as on her feet, clutching wildly at any bush to slow her speed. She began to run before she reached the level. A small landslide tumbled down the bluff behind her, unseen, as were the grass stains and rips in her clothing.

"Orvis!" She shouted as if he were human. "Orvis!"

He stopped. His turret rose and his lenses focused on her as she approached. Even in her excitement she remembered not to hurt herself by hugging him but patted the bowl of his turret with both hands, as if cradling a beloved face. "Orvis, I'm so glad to see you," she told him over and over. "I'm so glad to see you." She brushed her face quickly with her sleeves before he could see the tears in her eyes. "I didn't think you'd come. I thought you were off on your trip around the world."

"I am glad to see you." Orvis repeated her greeting. "I have learned I am no longer accustomed to being alone. I had never known what lonely was before. Does your great-grandmother need a used robot?"

"She asked about you right away," Toby said, glad that that was true, and not just a polite lie. "She'll be so happy to see you. And Thaddeus will be, too. He's still—"

"If she has no use for me I will return to the walled settlement."

"Why?" She stepped back to stare at him in surprise.

"Because I have been reviewing data as I walked. I do not frighten them. Several of them expressed pleasure at seeing me and said they remembered units like me. I could be of use to them. Also, there is a parallel between the space people and their village and myself and the Corona

Landfill. Like me they were high quality; they were used for space study; they aged and became obsolete. They are now in an isolated area where they will wear out unseen, until they cease to function. There is a difference in intelligence and strength. I am superior in both. I will not cease to function until long after the youngest of them does."

What Orvis was saying made sense in a way so sad that Toby didn't want to think about it too deeply. "But what would you do there?" she said.

"What I have always done. What humans cannot do but need done for them. In addition, I could be myself. Not a playmate or a toy. Not a hazard. I would be an old robot. But a useful old robot. What would I do for your great-grandmother?"

"She needs her library recatalogued, she said, and . . ." Suddenly remembering made Toby more enthusiastic about Orvis's plans. "She said that if they'd let her, she wanted to help the space people, too. You could work together."

"I am a multi-purpose robot. I would have purpose there."

"But I'd miss you."

"You and Thaddeus will not remain at this location. It is not your home."

". . . No," she admitted. "He can stay until spring break is over, to get rested, but then he has to go back to the Academy and I—I'll fight to stay, but if I lose, I have to transfer to a school on Mars."

"Because of Lillian."

"Yes, she—" Toby started to say and then giggled, startled that he had remembered.

"My memory contains data on schooling. I have scanned books on education. School is an inefficient system of programming human minds. Is that correct?"

". . . Yes." She'd never thought of it in quite that way.

"When you are sent to a new school, is that the human equivalent of being reprogrammed?"

"No. Yes . . . in a way. You might call it *adding data*."

"Why would adding data be termed a loss?"

"It isn't that. I don't want to leave Earth."

"Must you obey commands?" said Orvis. "Are children not free?"

She laughed. "Sometimes it feels like that. Most kids are. But they have to do what their parents tell them to do."

"Children are owned? Like robots?"

"No . . ." She wasn't sure. "At least I don't think so. Until we grow up we're responsible to our parents or Guardian. And they're responsible for us."

Orvis's lights blinked as he considered this, "*Responsible for* means a type of caring is implied?" he concluded.

"Usually. Yes." He was right. They did care, in their own way, by being responsible for her. Even Lillian.

"Would they continue to care for you if you were on Mars?" said Orvis.

". . . Yes."

"And you will be allowed to return from Mars if you are sent there?"

"Yes. In two years."

"Two years is a short time."

"For you, maybe," she said, suddenly irked by his objectivity. What would a robot know or care about saying good-bye, and two years spent where one didn't want to be? And then she remembered Orvis had just said he had learned what lonely meant. "Would you miss me?" she asked on impulse.

"If you mean 'Would I be aware of the lack of your presence,' yes. It would be a subtraction from my understanding of Home. I would also be aware of that lack if you were at the place you call the Academy, but in proportion to the time and distance between that site and Mars. I would accordingly lack Thaddeus less."

"You'd miss me more because I'd be farther away?"

Orvis had to translate this into his understanding. "Yes," he concluded.

"Thank you," she said, wishing there were some way to cross the barrier between a robot's understanding and her own. But then, she thought, it was almost as hard sometimes to cross the barrier between another person's understanding and her own. Skin was as effective as metal.

"So even if you do go back to help the villagers sometimes, this will still be your home." She pointed toward the dome of the big house.

"Your great-grandmother will be responsible for me?"

"Oh, yes. And in time you can be my robot—if you want to be."

"Thank you." Orvis's lenses scanned the shoreline, the bluff, and the human housing structure in the near distance. "Do you have any lemon bath oil in the house? I am unkempt. First impressions are important."

ABOUT THE AUTHOR

H. M. Hoover is one of America's leading writers of science fiction for young people. She is the author of *The Shepherd Moon, The Delikon, The Rains of Eridan, The Lost Star, Return to Earth*, and *This Time of Darkness*. Her book *Another Heaven, Another Earth* is an ALA Best Book for Young Adults.

Ms. Hoover lives near Washington, D.C., where she pursues her interests in natural history, archaeology, and history, as well as her writing.